For Cocoa, my sweet, beautiful dog who was with me through every book I've written.

THE DRAGON QUEEN

DARK WORLD: THE DRAGON TWINS 4

MICHELLE MADOW

DREAMSCAPE PUBLISHING

1

GEMMA

MONDAY, MAY 24 (PRESENT DAY)

I WOKE in Ethan's arms, my back toward him, with his body curled around mine. Warm, safe, and loved. This was where I belonged—with him. It was where I'd always belonged. I couldn't believe I'd ever doubted it.

I couldn't believe I'd ever thought he wasn't mine, and that I wasn't his.

We'd moved into the same quarters in Avalon's castle weeks ago, after learning that the life I'd lived while under the influence of the nightshade was real.

Sleeping beside him each night would have been perfect—if not for the fact that everything else in our lives was falling apart.

Mainly, the fact that my twin was lost to me.

I missed Mira so much that it physically hurt. I knew she was alive—I'd *feel* it if our twin bond was severed—

but not a day passed when I didn't wonder where she was, and how she was doing.

"Good morning," Ethan whispered in my ear, lulling me away from my worries about Mira. "How'd you sleep?"

"Good," I said, since I always slept well in Avalon. *Everyone* did. There was something in the water here—literally—that made our bodies function at their best at all times. Still, I loved that he always asked. "You?"

"Same," he said, and his hand wandered down my stomach, sending tingles through my body. "There's only one thing that could make this morning better."

His touch ignited the fire inside me. "And what's that?" I teased.

"I think you know *exactly* what it is." His voice turned low and husky, and I pressed myself back against him, smiling at the feel of how badly he wanted me.

Before we could continue, flames burst forth from the nightstand. They quickly disappeared, leaving a folded piece of parchment where they'd been.

"Ignore it," Ethan murmured, nibbling on the tip of my ear in a way that he knew drove me crazy. "We can look at it once we're finished here."

But I couldn't ignore it.

What if it had news about Mira?

I told him as much, and then I pushed myself up in bed, grabbed the message, and opened it.

It was from Harper.

I have new information about that thing I've been looking for. Get yourself to my room, ASAP.

See you soon,

-Your favorite witch/vampire/all-powerful user of magic

I showed the letter to Ethan, watching as he read it over.

Understanding crossed his hazel eyes at the realization that our relaxing morning together needed to get cut short.

"We have to go." I jumped out of bed and walked over to the wardrobe to get dressed.

Ethan did the same, and soon enough, we were both wearing our black Avalon Army uniforms. There was a bowl of mana on the coffee table, and I inhaled a piece of it quickly, not wanting to be hungry during this meeting with Harper.

I could never focus when I was hungry.

This morning, the mana tasted like one of my favorites—pancakes with maple syrup. I washed it down with some holy water, and then was ready to go.

Once finished, Ethan and I walked to the door together and reached for the keys hanging from our necklaces. We never took them off—not even while sleeping.

Lastly, I reached into the ether, pulled out the Holy Crown, and placed it on my head. There was no need to wear it in front of Harper, but I liked to make an entrance. Plus, with Ethan by my side and the Holy Crown on my head, I felt braver.

Stronger.

Ready for whatever the universe threw my way.

I slipped my key into the keyhole, opened the door, and stepped into the ivory hall of Hecate's Eternal Library. The tall, rounded ceiling carved with swirling patterns of flowers looked the same as always.

But, per usual, Hecate wasn't waiting at the other side of the hall. I released a sigh of disappointment. I hadn't expected to see her there, and I hadn't entered the Library with the goal of speaking with her, but there were still always questions I wanted to ask.

The door closed behind me, then it opened again, and Ethan stepped through. He glanced across the hall, also unsurprised not to see Hecate.

Then he stared down at me, his eyes hungry. "Whatever Harper has to tell us better be important," he said. "Because I was *not* done with you this morning."

My cheeks heated, and I stepped up on my toes to plant a soft kiss on his lips. He groaned and pulled me closer, but I stepped back, my eyes teasing. "Good," I said. "Because I certainly wasn't done with you, either."

We shared a special, secretive smile—the kind that only existed between two people in love. Soulmates. Or, in our case, twin flames.

Then, not wanting to risk getting carried away, I spun around, placed my key back into the lock, and stepped through the door into Harper's room in the Vale.

2

GEMMA

MONDAY, MAY 24 (PRESENT DAY)

Harper was pacing around in her palatial room, waiting for us. Her boyfriend Rohan sat at the table next to the huge window that overlooked the snow-covered mountains, picking at a bowl of fruit. Because the Vale was west of Avalon—nestled in the Canadian Rocky Mountains—it was the dead of night here.

"Finally." Harper let out a relieved breath and stopped pacing. "Took you long enough."

"We were just waking up," I explained, unable to meet her eyes. If I did, she'd totally know what Ethan and I had been up to when she'd sent the fire message.

"Good. Because I had a breakthrough about the Dark Sword. I was finally able to get an answer to a question I needed to ask." She played with the key around her neck, making it clear what she meant—Hecate had appeared to her in the Library. "It led me to some new information, and this morning, it led me to this."

She walked over to her bed, where a large hardcover book lay open to a page in the center. She picked it up and thrust it into my arms. "Here. Check it out."

I glanced at the chapter title, which simply said *The RMS Titanic: Maiden Voyage*.

"What's this?" I asked.

"It's a ship that was a big deal in the early twentieth century," she said. "It took people back and forth from England to New York."

"What does it have to do with the Dark Sword?"

"I was able to track the Sword down to a shifter who boarded that ship for its maiden voyage," she said. "I don't know the shifter's name, but she got on the ship with the Sword in England. There's no record of her since. Which means you have to go back and find her there."

I glanced at the dates of the Titanic's maiden voyage. April 10-17, 1912.

If Harper was correct—which I was sure she was—then I'd be going back to the turn of the twentieth century. Over a hundred years ago. It would be the furthest I'd traveled back in time yet.

The world had been so different back then. How was I supposed to fit in?

But that was a question for later. First, we needed a basic game plan.

"So we should go back to before the Titanic left England," I said. "Find the shifter and get the Dark Sword before she can set sail with it."

"Not possible," Harper said. "I only know that she boarded the ship. I don't know where she was before she got on it."

"Okay," I took a deep breath and thought through it. "So we'll go to New York on April 17. Wait for her to get off the ship, then grab her, steal the Sword, and bring it back to the present."

"Except I don't know *who* she is," Harper said. "You won't know who you're looking for. The moment she leaves the city—which could be immediately after her arrival—we'll be back to square one. And we both know that the dragon heart you used all those weeks ago in Antarctica doesn't have enough juice left in it to track the Sword through the city. It'll be a miracle if it can track the Sword on the ship."

Dread swirled in my stomach at the obvious solution—the one I was trying to avoid.

"We need to go *on* the ship," Ethan said, and nausea hit me just from thinking about it.

After how seasick I'd gotten during the Antarctica journey, I'd sworn never to go on another cruise again.

But shifters couldn't teleport. Assuming this shifter wasn't traveling with a witch—which was probably a correct assumption, given that the different supernatural species hadn't been on good terms with each other in the early twentieth century—she'd be cornered once we found her. And Ethan and I were far more powerful than a shifter. We'd just have to fight her, steal the Dark Sword, escape with it through the Eternal Library, and bring it back to the present.

It was nothing I couldn't handle. Especially with Ethan by my side.

"Exactly my thought," Harper said. "And don't worry—there are herbs that help with motion sickness. I can easily brew up a potion for you."

"Thanks." It would have to be a miracle potion, but I'd try anything.

"So," Rohan said, eyeing us up. "What do the two of you know about life in 1912?"

"Nothing." I shrugged. "Other than that the women had to wear dresses. And corsets. And... well, I guess that's it."

"You're going to have to know a lot more than that if you don't want to draw attention in the past," he said. "And that's the goal, correct? Create the fewest number of changes possible?"

"That's right," I said, since the fewer changes we

made, the less likely it would be that one of them would butterfly out and create a change that stopped one of the Queens who'd already gotten an Object from acquiring it. If that happened, Time would reject the change, and we wouldn't have a second chance to get back on that ship, since I could only travel back to the same time once. "But you were alive in 1912, right?"

"In 1912, I was living in India," he said. "Life there was extremely different than it was in Europe. I'm not sure how much I'd be able to help you."

"Then I guess we'll have to find another vampire to help us—one that lived in Europe in 1912," I said. "And given all the connections we have, it shouldn't be hard to find one."

3

GEMMA

TUESDAY, MAY 25 (PRESENT DAY)

NOAH, Jacen, and Annika immediately knew the perfect vampire to help us. So the next day, Ethan and I headed to the Haven, ready and excited to meet her.

She waited in the tearoom, and she was drinking a cup of coffee. She had pale skin, dark hair, and light blue eyes. If her scent wasn't the distinct metallic one of a vampire, I might have thought she was a Foster witch.

She placed her cup down on the coffee table, stood, and curtseyed. "Queen Gemma," she said, her gaze lowered to the floor. "King Pendragon."

"Princess Karina," I said. "Please rise."

I smiled inwardly, feeling like I was getting the hang of this whole "being royal" thing.

She did as I asked.

"You can call me Gemma," I said, since no matter

how royal I was, I felt a lot more comfortable with people once the formalities were dropped.

She nodded, and since I was of higher rank than she, it was a given that I could drop her title, too.

"And 'Ethan' is a lot less of a mouthful than 'King Pendragon,'" Ethan said, and Karina gave him a small smile at that.

We sat down and helped ourselves to coffee. The holy water on Avalon was refreshing, but it had nothing on real coffee.

"Harper and Rohan briefed me on your mission," Karina said. "And my friends on Avalon were correct—I'm the perfect vampire to help you. Not only did I live in Europe during the time you're visiting, but I've always had an interest in ships. And I just happen to have traveled on a similar voyage from Europe to America on one of the Titanic's sister ships, the Olympic."

"So you'll help us," I said.

"That's why I'm here."

"Good." I smiled, relieved, even though I'd already figured as much. "Where should we start?"

"Easy," she said, looking me up and down. "If you're going to fit in while we're in 1912, we're going to have to get you some appropriate clothing."

4

GEMMA

TUESDAY, JUNE 1 (PRESENT DAY)

Six days had passed in the present.

During that time—thanks to the magic of time travel—we'd spent two weeks in 1912 leading up to the day we'd be traveling to today. And I didn't know what we would have done without Karina, since her vampire compulsion, along with her knowledge of the time period, had proved extraordinarily useful.

She'd gotten us a hotel room in Southampton, which was where we'd be boarding the ship. She'd given us a run-down on what we'd need to know regarding etiquette of the era, and had gotten us fitted for clothes so we'd have everything we needed for the journey.

And we needed a *lot* of clothes. The women on board first class—which was where we'd be traveling, since it would give us access to most anywhere on the ship we pleased—apparently changed their dresses at *least* four times a day. It was ridiculous, but if I didn't do it, I might draw unwanted attention from the other passengers on board. So, Karina had gotten me a month's worth of clothing for a five-day voyage.

I was going to have to spend more time changing outfits than searching for the shifter.

Then there were the hats. They were huge, and so covered with feathers that it was like wearing a bird on my head. To make things worse, women were expected to wear gloves at all times. It took me a lot of tries (and a lot of destroyed gloves) to figure out how to use my fire magic without burning them.

But that wasn't close to the worst of it. Because in the evening, I was expected to wear a corset. AKA one of the worst torture devices known to women. And even though Torrence had a signature family spell that could make any piece of clothing fit perfectly, a perfectly fit corset was *meant* to be suffocating. So the spell did absolutely nothing to help.

Along with clothing, Karina also managed to acquire fake identities for me and Ethan. We'd be traveling as a married couple, given the scandal that would emerge if passengers saw as much as a romantic glance between the two of us otherwise. Karina would be traveling as Ethan's sister. And, luckily for us, forty percent of the

Titanic's first-class suites were listed as empty in the manifest, so it was easy for Karina to book us one of those.

Now, we were standing in a back alley in Southampton in the present day, dressed in clothes appropriate for 1912. I didn't feel particularly ready to blend into the time period, but the longer we spent preparing in the present, the more time Lilith had to track down the Dark Sword.

If she found the Dark Sword and got it into the hands of the future Dark Queen of Swords, then Time would lock in the Dark Queen of Swords' fate, and there'd be nothing we could do to change it.

"You ready to get this over with?" Karina asked.

"Ready as I'll ever be," I said, and then I took her hands, told the Crown to bring us to April 10, 1912, and we flickered back through time.

5

GEMMA

WEDNESDAY, APRIL 10, 1912

I DROPPED Karina off in the alley—which had the same exposed brick wall in 1912 as it did in the current day—then returned to the present, grabbed Ethan, and brought him back as well.

I stashed the Crown back into the ether, and we emerged from the alley onto the main street. The air smelled smoggier than it did in the present, which continued to shock me every time we traveled back here.

We passed three women wearing similar hats to the ones Karina and I had on. A man rode by on a bike, and a trolly made its way down the rails in the center of the street. None of them paid us much attention as we walked down the sidewalk toward the hotel we'd been staying in.

Karina had gotten us a two-bedroom suite, and our luggage was in the living room where we'd left it.

She glanced at the clock on the mantle. "Our car should be here by now," she said. "Are you guys ready?"

"As I'll ever be." I took a deep breath and looked to Ethan, who nodded as if saying, *we've got this.*

Preemptively, I reached into my bag for one of the vials with the light orange anti-seasick potion Harper had given me, and took a swig. It tasted like ginger, and tingled going down.

Karina picked up the antique phone on the desk, rang the lobby, and asked them to send the bellboys up for our luggage.

"It's so frustrating to watch them moving our things when the three of us are far stronger than they are," she said with a sigh. "But we must maintain appearances."

That was the mantra of this journey.

Maintain appearances.

The bellboys came for our luggage and took it down the back steps to the lobby.

As Karina had said, a black buggy was in front of the hotel waiting for us. The bellboys placed our luggage on the *top* of the car and strapped it in, and I prayed it wouldn't fall.

Not that I would mind those corsets getting lost in the street.

The driver opened the car door, and Karina and I got in first, followed by Ethan. The inside was small and cramped, but luckily, we didn't have to go far.

As we approached the port, there was a parade of cars on the street. Most had luggage on the top—I assumed they were also full of people preparing to board the Titanic. Many of them would be putting their cars in the Titanic's cargo section to bring with them to America.

We turned a corner around the buildings, and the ship came into view.

The Titanic was one of the largest, grandest ships in the world in 1912. A huge crowd of onlookers had gathered around the port simply to admire it and watch it set sail.

But I had to admit—compared to modern day cruise ships, it was rather small. It must have been half the size of the Golden Moon—the ship we'd taken to Antarctica—and the Golden Moon wasn't nearly as large as some of the mega ships that existed in the present.

"My, how times have changed," Karina said, and I had a feeling she was thinking the same thing.

Our driver yelled at the onlookers to make way, and the crowd parted to let us pass. Most of them were dressed in simpler clothes than we wore, and they craned their necks to try to see inside the car, as if we were celebrities. We had to drive at a snail's pace to make sure not to run anyone over.

Finally, we arrived at the gangway. Karina showed our tickets to the crewmen waiting for us, and they sent a group to tag our bags to have them sent to our room. Then, a steward dressed in finery fitting to serve first-class passengers led us on board and to our suite: B88.

We walked inside, and I immediately retracted my thought about the ship being unimpressive. Because our suite on the Golden Sea—which was one of the most luxurious cruise lines in the present—was bare bones compared to this one. This suite was *ornate*, with paneled wooden walls, velvet canopy beds, a fireplace, crystal lamps, and a full sitting area with plush sofas and chairs. It was like it had been designed for royalty, and it was large enough to host a small party.

"Well," I said as I looked around. "We certainly have enough space to change into all those dresses."

"Back in the day, we traveled in style." Karina's cheeks glowed, as if she felt at home in this time long past. "And this isn't even the largest suite on board."

There was a knock on the door, and a steward delivered the luggage. "Shall I leave these in the servants' quarters?" he asked, and he looked around, as if searching for our servant—which we didn't have.

If he thought this was odd, he said nothing.

"Please," Karina said, and the steward dropped the trunks off in the least lavish room in the suite.

Next, he presented us with a booklet that explained what we should expect on the trip, and a first-class passenger list to browse. Providing the passenger list seemed strange, but I supposed many of them knew each other and would like to know which of their friends were on board.

"Is there anything else I can assist you with?" he asked.

"We're fine for now," Karina said, and once he left, she turned back to me and Ethan. "Time to get started. So how about we head out to the Boat Deck and keep watch for that shifter?"

"Let's do it," I said, and Ethan and I followed her out of the room, ready to nab the shifter and get back to the present as soon as possible.

6

GEMMA

WEDNESDAY, APRIL 10, 1912

The Titanic's layout was nearly identical to the Olympic's—the ship Karina had previously sailed on—so she was easily able to lead us to the Boat Deck. It was the deck where the lifeboats were stored, but more importantly, it was the largest outdoor space for first class passengers to spend time on. It was full of people who'd gathered to take a stroll, mingle, and search the crowd at the dock for any family members who were seeing them off.

On our stroll, we did a preliminarily look-over of the other first-class passengers to see if any of them smelled of shifter. We doubted they would—a shifter traveling with the Dark Sword would likely have a crystal to cloak their scent—but it didn't hurt to check.

Our assumption that we wouldn't be able to simply sniff them out proved correct.

After about an hour of walking around, the Titanic sounded its steam engines, and we were off. I braced myself on the rails, preparing myself for the jolt.

But as we pulled away from port, a miracle happened.

My stomach didn't experience those first cramps of motion sickness.

I was seriously going to have to thank Harper for that potion when we got back.

"You okay?" Ethan asked me.

"Yeah," I said, surprised. "I'm good."

"You look good."

I smiled and felt my cheeks heat. "Thanks."

As the ship left port, we waved to the crowd, even though we knew no one out there. As long as we had the opportunity to live in history, we might as well enjoy it.

Eventually, we were out in the open ocean, and passengers started leaving the deck.

"Everyone is likely going to explore the facilities," Karina said. "Let's head back to our cabin, change, then do the same."

"Do we have to change?" I muttered.

"Do you want to be seen again in the same dress you wore for sail away?" she asked, and she spun around, not waiting for an answer before leading the way back to our suite.

We didn't see anyone who might be a shifter while exploring the first-class areas of the ship, and I was getting the feeling that this mission was going to be harder than we'd hoped.

A bugle sounded in early evening, while we were having tea in the lounge to keep an eye on the other passengers.

Karina set down her teacup and stood up. "Time to change for dinner," she said.

"Did they sound the bugle to let us know it was time to change for dinner?" I asked.

What was this—summer camp?

"Correct," she said, and then we followed her back to the room to change. I had her tie my corset as loosely as she deemed socially acceptable, and even then, it barely felt like I could breathe.

"What am I supposed to do if we find the shifter and need to fight her?" I asked. "I'll hardly be of any use if I can't catch my breath."

"Fine," Karina said, and she loosened the corset further. It wasn't perfect, but at least I no longer felt like

I was suffocating. "We'll let the others think you might be pregnant."

"You think I look pregnant?" My jaw dropped at the insult.

"Of course not," she said. "But it would explain the loosened corset."

I pursed my lips and glared at her.

"At least it won't cause a scandal," Ethan said. "Since they think we're married."

My heart fluttered at the thought of being married to Ethan, even though the documents had been forged.

Not that marriage mattered to us. The twin flame bond was far stronger than any paper contract.

Ethan held his arm out for me at the top of a gorgeous grand staircase with a stunning clock in the center. "Shall we?" he asked with a twinkle in his eyes.

In his tailor-made suit, he looked like a perfect gentleman. No one would have guessed that he was capable of shifting into a dragon and shooting so much fire out of his mouth that he could burn down this entire ship.

"Of course," I said, and I linked my arm with his, and we made our way down the staircase.

Light poured through the glass dome overhead, and I felt like a movie star going to a swanky party. I'd already walked down the grand staircase, since it could access nearly all the first-class facilities, but it was far more stunning when everyone was dressed like they were attending a fairy tale ball.

The reception room was at the bottom, and we walked through it into the dining saloon. A string quintet played music in the background, along with a pianist, and I relished the luxury.

This was so different from my normal life, and while I felt insanely out of place, I was enjoying it at the same time. Luckily, there were far more important people on board for the other passengers to bother mingling with us, which was ideal, since we needed to affect history as little as possible.

Dinner was an insane, *ten course,* three-hour affair. I'd never been into fancy food—I'd take pizza or a burger any day—and as I ate, I thought how much Harper would love this. She was the biggest foodie I knew.

Maybe one day, after we won the war against the demons, I'd take her on another sailing of the Titanic so she could experience it herself. On the condition that she made me another batch of seasickness potion.

"Do we have to do this every night?" I asked Karina as the servers took away our ninth course. As supernaturals, we had faster metabolisms than humans, but this was a lot of food, even for me.

It was also taking forever.

"Dinner is one of our best opportunities to listen in on other people's conversations," she said, and I sighed, since it was true. With our supernatural hearing, we were able to listen to people in the tables around us, although they were mainly gossiping about the other passengers on board. It was similar to the talk in high school cafeterias, except with expensive food and way fancier outfits.

There was absolutely zero talk about anything that might give us a clue about who the shifter was, or the location of the Dark Sword.

After dinner, we lingered in the reception room, walking around to eavesdrop some more. Again, we heard nothing useful. Finally, the hall closed, and we were able to return to the suite and change into our pajamas.

"What's the plan for tomorrow?" I asked after we were ready for bed. "Head down to second class and see if we can learn anything useful there?"

"Many of the passengers who boarded in France missed dinner tonight," Karina said, referring to the stop the Titanic made after Southampton to pick up its final group of passengers. "We'll spend tomorrow in first class again to see if we pick up anything useful from them. Plus, today was only half a day. As we saw while exploring, there are many amenities to enjoy in first class tomorrow."

"Is this a mission or a vacation?" I asked, since it was sure sounding like she was treating it as the latter.

"Both," she said, and then she turned off the lights, retired to her room, and we went to sleep.

7

GEMMA

THURSDAY, APRIL 11, 1912

THE NEXT MORNING AFTER BREAKFAST, we walked the first-class halls, with Ethan carrying the shriveled dragon heart in his jacket pocket. The idea was that if the dragon heart was close enough to a room with the Dark Sword inside, it would be able to detect the Sword, so we could get on with our mission.

Either the Dark Sword wasn't in any of the first-class suites, or the dragon heart was out of juice, because we found nothing.

After a walk past the final first-class suite, we headed back to our suite to change for tea. Because of course, it would be totally appalling to wear the same dress to tea that I'd worn to breakfast.

Tea was in the first-class lounge, which was one of the most ornate rooms on the ship. It reminded me of the palace at the Vale, which Harper had told me was decorated to resemble the Versailles palace in France.

We sat down in the plush armchairs at one of the center tables, since it gave us the best chance to listen in on the surrounding conversations. But, as we drank our tea and made light conversation while we eavesdropped, my eyes kept wandering to the beautiful, fully stocked wooden bookcase at the opposite side of the room.

"Go take a look," Ethan said to me. "Karina and I have things covered over here."

I quickly put down my cup of tea and made my way over to the bookshelves. I recognized a bunch of books in there, including *Wuthering Heights, Jane Eyre, Vanity Fair,* and some of my favorites by Jane Austen. I also couldn't help but be amused at the sight of *The Time Machine* by HG Wells.

I was examining the *Anne of Green Gables* collection when someone stepped up next to me.

"Are you a fan of LM Montgomery?" the woman asked.

She was beautiful, with pale skin, dark hair, and soft features. Her dress wasn't as tight around the waist as the other women, and at closer inspection, she appeared to be pregnant.

She was also wearing so much jewelry that I was surprised she wasn't sinking the ship.

"I love *Anne of Green Gables*," I said, although another book near it caught my attention a second later. "But *The Secret Garden* has been one of my favorites since I was a kid."

She studied me for a moment, then let out a lively laugh. "How could you have read it as a kid?" she asked. "It's brand new."

"Oh." I bit my lower lip at the blunder. "I must have confused it with something else."

"Well, if you haven't read it, then you should," she said. "It truly is fantastic."

"I will." I smiled, glad she hadn't pressed further. "Thank you."

"Are you from Australia?"

"Yes," I said, relieved for the change of subject. "Have you been?"

I internally cursed myself for asking, since I doubted anyone on this ship had been to Australia. It wasn't particularly easy to get to in the early 1900s, and in 1912, it hadn't been that long since Australia was the place where the British had sent their convicts.

Then again, she'd recognized my accent. And she was clearly rich. So maybe it wasn't *too* crazy of a thought that she'd been there.

"Not yet," she said. "But my husband has an itch to go. I'm sure we'll make it there someday." She pulled *The*

Secret Garden off the shelves and handed it to me. "Take it. I'm sure it'll make you feel like a child again."

"Thanks," I said, and as I examined the pristine hardback, I couldn't help but think about how tempting it would be to take this beautiful first edition back with me to the present.

"My pleasure." She removed another book from the shelves—*The Autobiography of Benjamin Franklin*—and pranced back with it to her table. It was one of the larger tables in the room, and she sat in the center of the sofa that was surrounded by a group of women. They cleared space for her, and from the way they were focused on her, she seemed to be the most popular one in the group.

I clutched the copy of *The Secret Garden* to my chest and walked back to where I'd been sitting with Karina and Ethan.

As I sat down, Karina looked at me like I'd done something extraordinary.

"What?" I asked, since she clearly wanted to say something.

"Do you know who that woman is that you were talking to?"

"You know how many friends I have here in 1912," I said sarcastically. "Who is she?"

She leaned closer, lowered her voice, and said,

"That's Madeline Astor. She's the wife of the richest man in the world—John Astor. They love to travel. They're returning back home to America after a long tour of Egypt."

"She mentioned that her husband wanted to visit Australia," I said, and then I realized I knew who they were. Well, at least I knew who *he* was. "They end up going. The street I lived on is John Astor Road, and I went to John Astor High. Tons of things in Australia are named after him."

"Now that you mention it, I remember hearing about their journey there," she said, and then she looked to the book in my hand. "What do you plan on doing with that?"

"Reading it," I said. What else did someone do with a book?

"I suppose you'll have some time to read after we find the Dark Sword," she said, since we had to wait to time travel back to the present until we reached New York. If I tried to bring her to the present while we were on board, we'd end up in the middle of the ocean. "But it would be a shame to miss a minute of this once-in-a-lifetime experience because your nose is buried in a book."

"That's Gemma's favorite place for her nose to be," Ethan said, which earned a smile from me.

"It is," I said. "But Karina's right. We should make the most of this experience. I can always read once we're back home."

"You're taking the book back with you?" From Karina's tone, it was obvious she disapproved.

"Yep."

"What about everything you said about making the fewest changes in the past possible?"

"It's one book." I shrugged. "It'll be fine. Plus, I'm the Queen of Pentacles. If I want to bring the book back with me, then that's what I'm going to do."

8

GEMMA

SUNDAY, APRIL 14, 1912

ON FRIDAY, we did the same thing in second class that we'd done in first class—had dinner, eavesdropped on passengers in common areas, and walked by each cabin with the dragon heart to see if it sensed the Dark Sword.

Just like in first class, we finished as clueless as we'd started.

On Saturday, Karina compelled the crew to let us into the cargo area of the ship. There was a *lot* of cargo, and we meticulously searched through each item.

No Dark Sword.

On Sunday morning, there was supposed to be a lifeboat drill, which we thought would be a good opportunity to do a more thorough check of the passengers in case we'd missed some. But the captain canceled it. So we spent the day in steerage, doing the same thing there that we'd done in first and second class.

Nothing turned up.

And Hecate wasn't in the Eternal Library any of those days to answer our questions.

Now, we were back in our suite after dinner, changing into our night robes and trying to figure out our next move.

"The dragon heart is worthless," I said, looking at the shriveled heart in frustration. "We might as well throw it into the ocean for all the good it's been doing us."

"There's still a bit of life left in it," Ethan said. "Not much, but it should have been able to help us."

I shook my head, since if the heart still had life in it, it sure didn't look like it to me.

"I have a question, and you might not like it," Karina said, and we looked at her to continue. "What if Harper was wrong? What if the Dark Sword isn't on this ship?"

"Harper wasn't wrong," I said.

"How can you know for sure?"

"Because she asked Hecate in the Eternal Library."

Of course, since Karina wasn't a witch and didn't have a key, what I'd said went completely over her head.

"So her source was a good one," she said instead.

"Yes," I answered. "Exactly."

She easily accepted this, thanks to the magic of Hecate's keys.

We were sitting around the fireplace—which was actually fake, since a real one would be a fire hazard—when I felt a shift. It was like the world was being pulled apart and pieced back together again.

I *knew* this feeling.

It was the same feeling I'd gotten when I'd watched Katherine change my and Ethan's memories in the cove.

But Katherine was currently in a deep sleep in a cabin below the Antarctic Circle. This wasn't because of her. And there was only one other person in the world who could do something like this.

"Gemma?" Ethan asked. "What's wrong?"

"Mira's here," I said. "And she's making a change in the timeline. A *big* change."

"How can you tell?" Karina asked.

"Because I can feel it."

"So, you can feel where she is?"

"No," I said, and then I looked to Ethan. "Does that heart definitely have some life left in it?"

"Yes," he said. "I'm sure of it."

"Good." I picked the heart up from the coffee table, closed my eyes, and focused on Mira.

She was my twin. Our souls were connected. More than that—our magical objects were connected.

I reached into the ether, removed the Holy Crown, and placed it on my head. The moment I did, its magic flowed through me, filling me with confidence.

The heart didn't have enough power left in it to take me to the Dark Sword. But maybe…

I gathered as much magic as I could, closed my eyes, and pushed it into the dragon heart, like a burst of energy to bring it back to life.

Take me to the Dark Crown, I thought.

The heart pulsed with energy, and an image flashed through my mind.

Mira, on the Titanic, in one of the places I'd been with Karina and Ethan.

When I opened my eyes, Karina and Ethan were staring at me in shock.

The dragon heart in my hands was gray and dead.

"What did you see?" Ethan asked.

"I know where Mira is," I said, and I hurried out the door, not even bothering to put on my shoes before leaving the suite.

9

GEMMA

SUNDAY, APRIL 14, 1912

WE PASSED two first-class passengers in the hall, and they watched us run by in our nightclothes, their mouths wide open at what I supposed to them was a massive scandal.

Not wanting to run into any more passengers, I took a flight of stairs up to the deck below the Boat Deck—the A Deck—and hurried down the first class promenade toward the front of the ship. The outside decks were empty, since it was so freezing outside that the humans preferred to stay indoors. Luckily, vampires had a high tolerance for cold, as did Ethan and I, thanks to our fire magic.

At the front of the deck, I saw her. Mira. She was three decks below, on D Deck which was open space for the steerage passengers. She stood at the railing, carrying a tan woman with wild dark curls. The woman flopped in Mira's arms, looking either unconscious or dead. They both wore the simple clothing of steerage passengers.

A charcoal-colored sword that I assumed was the Dark Sword lay next to my twin's feet.

I hurried down the three decks to D Deck in time to watch Mira hoist the woman over the railing and toss her out to sea.

Mira placed her hands on the railing and looked over it, like she was checking to make sure her job was complete. That woman had to be the shifter. Then, still facing the ocean, Mira reached down and picked up the Sword.

All she needed to do was go to a door, use her key to enter the Eternal Library, and disappear to anywhere in the world.

I needed to stop her before she had the chance.

"Block the doors," I told Ethan and Karina, and then I ran forward, meeting Mira's eyes as the turned to look at me.

She scowled, her eyes full of hate, and she held the Sword at the ready.

But Mira didn't excel in swordplay. She was strongest with her elements.

I reached inside myself to connect to my fire magic,

but I didn't call it forward. The light would bring attention to us, and I didn't want any humans to check on what was going on and get caught in the crossfire.

"You shouldn't have come," Mira said, and ice crawled out of her hands and up the Sword, turning it into a frozen weapon.

"You can't use that," I said. "You're not the Dark Queen of Swords."

"Its magic won't connect with me, but I can still use it like a regular sword." She leaped toward me, ready to attack, but was blown back by a gust of wind so strong that it slammed her to the floor.

Ethan.

I glanced over my shoulder, and sure enough, Ethan stood in front of one of the doors, palms out and ready to help me against Mira's attacks.

"It's three against one," I said as she pushed herself back up. "You can't beat us."

Her eyes darted around, landing on each of us. She was cornered, and she knew it.

Which made this the perfect time to tell her the truth.

"Do you remember when I was poisoned by the nightshade on Moon Mountain?" I asked her.

She stared at me, Sword out in front of her, not moving.

"I had a vision," I continued. "Of the original version of the past. In it, Ethan and I were together from that first day we met in the cove."

"There were no alternate versions of the past back then," she snarled. "Neither of us had gotten our magic yet."

"Neither one of *us* had our magic yet," I said. "But there was someone else who could change the past as we knew it."

Wind swirled around her, although she made no move to attack again.

"I went to the Eternal Library and asked Hecate about the vision," I continued. "I learned that Katherine, Constance, Isemay, and Genevieve didn't wake from their sleep right before we got to Antarctica. They woke months earlier, on the day before our birthday. Constance had a vision strong enough to pull them out of the spell. She saw us getting our magic the next day, and she saw the griffin kill you."

"Her vision was clearly wrong."

"It wasn't," I said. "Because in the vision, Ethan and I were together. He ran after me when the griffin attacked instead of bringing you to the cave. You were standing on the beach, unprotected, when the griffin attacked."

"No." Her grip tightened around the handle of the

Sword, and the wind picked up around her. "He wouldn't do that. He *didn't* do that."

"You're right—he didn't do that," I said. "Katherine and the others in the Seventh Kingdom knew they needed to stop it from happening. They knew one of us was destined to become the Queen of Pentacles, and they needed to keep us both alive. So Katherine went to the cove when Ethan and I were spending time there the night before the ceremony. She used her compulsion on us. She told us that on the day Ethan and I met, he didn't stay with me in the cove. He went on, found you, and ended up dating you. And you know how Katherine's gift of compulsion works. It didn't just change my and Ethan's memories. It changed the memories of everyone connected to us, so we *all* believed that a past that never happened was real."

"You're lying."

"I'm not. Ask Hecate the next time you're in the Eternal Library."

She glanced at Ethan, heartbreak splattered across her face, and then she hurled the Dark Sword at me like a javelin.

I dove out of the way a split second before it could pierce through my heart.

It clanked as it hit the floor, and Ethan bolted toward

it. He picked it up, sprinted back to the door he'd been guarding, and used his key to go through.

He and the Sword were gone. He was in the Library, waiting for me to join him, pick a new destination, and bring us back to the present.

But I couldn't leave. Not when I'd finally found Mira.

Plus, I needed to stop her from following him into the Library.

So I spun back around to face my twin. Her palms faced up toward the night sky, creating an arch of ice over her head. The ice crept along her arms, icicles growing from the bottoms of them, and traveled along her entire body. She looked like a frozen sculpture. But still, she could move.

She raised her hands, palms toward me, and sharp icicles grew out of each one.

I still didn't call my fire. I just stood there, eyes locked with hers, waiting.

"Do it," I challenged. "Kill me."

She sneered. "You're not even going to try to fight me?"

"You're my twin," I said simply. "Hurting you is the same as hurting myself."

Wind howled around the deck, and my hair whipped across my cheeks. But I refused to leave her there. I'd already lost her once—I couldn't bear losing her again.

So I stood strong, staring her down, daring her to do it. The ice continued to grow out of her, and the wind blew stronger.

As the seconds passed, doubt crept inside me. Because Mira was the Dark Queen of Pentacles. And I'd seen Torrence when she'd been fully dark, right after Selena had been killed in front of her.

She hadn't been affected by her best friend's death.

I loved my twin. But as much as I wanted to believe that Mira was mentally stronger than Torrence, I knew it wasn't true.

Time felt like it slowed around us, and I braced myself for Mira's attack. I wanted to close my eyes, but I didn't.

Because if my twin was going to kill me, then I wanted her to be looking me in the eyes when she did it.

10

GEMMA

SUNDAY, APRIL 14, 1912

MIRA'S FACE contorted in pain, like she was having an intense internal battle.

Then she spun around to face the front of the ship and released her magic into the ocean with a loud scream.

The ice kept coming out of her palms, like there was a bottomless pit of it inside her. Finally, when it seemed impossible for there to be any more magic left, she released the last bit of it and collapsed to the floor.

As she sat up, I ran to her side and wrapped my arms around her in a hug.

She didn't flinch out of my embrace.

But I couldn't focus on her. Because there was something *growing* out of the ocean where she'd thrown her magic. A shadow in the dark night, building on itself until it was taller than it was wide.

The ship sailed closer toward it, and fear formed in my throat at the realization of what we were seeing.

"Iceberg, straight ahead!" a male voice called out from one of the watchpoints behind us.

The ship groaned as it tried to maneuver its way around the giant block of ice, but the iceberg was too close. The Titanic had no chance.

Without some supernatural interference, we were going to hit it.

"Use your magic to melt it," I told Mira.

She raised her hands, but nothing came out.

"I can't." She dropped her arms back to her sides. "I'm drained."

I held up my hands and shot bursts of fire out of my palms. But there was so much ice. Too much for me to melt.

I barely made a dent before the bottom of the ship collided with the ice below the water. A painfully loud screech filled the air as ice tore through steel.

Mira and I stared up at the iceberg and gaped as we passed by. At some point, Karina had run forward to stand next to us, and she was staring at it, too.

Chunks of ice broke off and fell onto the deck.

The screech of ice against steel continued for so long that the sound would be ingrained in my mind forever.

Others hurried out to the deck—curious passengers who wanted to see what had happened. Their eyes were wide as we passed the iceberg and left it behind.

This was bad.

Really, really bad.

We weren't supposed to change history. But now...

"You need to go with Ethan to the Library," Mira said. "Bring him back to the present and get the Sword to Avalon."

I stared at her, shocked. "You're talking like you're on our side."

"I *am* on your side," she said. "Lilith and Lavinia used transformation potion so I didn't know who they were, and they tricked me into going with them to their lair. Lilith is the Dark Queen of Cups. She used the Dark Grail to bind me to her, and she's been controlling my mind ever since."

"Is she in your mind now?"

"Sort of," she said. "The further back in time I go, the less control she has over me. It's like the gap in time weakens her hold. And just now—when I made the choice to save you instead of kill you—I weakened the bond. But it's still there, lingering in the back of my mind. If I return to the present, it'll take full control again."

"So you're staying here," I said. "Until we kill Lilith and break that bond."

"Yes."

"Then I'm staying with you."

"No," she said. "They need you in the present to win the war against Lilith and the demons. You have to stop her from completing her ultimate goal."

"Raising Lucifer," I said.

"How did you know?"

"Skylar saw it in a vision a few weeks ago."

"She's right," Mira said, even though we both knew Skylar's visions were never wrong. "Lilith needs fresh gifted vampire blood to raise Lucifer. She's been turning gifted humans into vampires since the demons rose from Hell, and she's been collecting their blood for the spell to free him from his prison realm there."

"But you said she needs *fresh* gifted vampire blood," I said. "Most of that blood is years old."

"Which is why she needed me," Mira said.

"She's been sending you back in time to bring the blood to the present," I realized.

"Yes."

"Which means she knew what the Holy and Dark Crowns could do all along."

"She did. And I refuse to go back to the present to be her slave again. But once you kill her, I'll feel the bond break. I'll return to the present, go through the Angel Trials, and find you on Avalon."

"You're a Dark Queen," I said. "You don't know if you'll pass the Angel Trials."

She narrowed her eyes, and they flashed icy blue. "I'm going to pass the Angel Trials."

I didn't argue with her, since if she tried to pass the Trials and failed, she'd end up in the river that led to the Vale. If that happened, Harper or someone else who lived there would let me know Mira was there.

"You can't stay here in 1912 alone," I said instead, and I looked up to Karina, who was standing there, listening to us. "Will you stay with her and make sure she's okay here?"

"Of course I will," she said. "Once we dock in New York, I'll get us situated there until everything is figured out in the present."

"This ship isn't docking in New York." Mira picked up a piece of ice and stared at it vacantly.

"What do you mean?" Karina asked.

"The ice ripped through the steel. Right now, water is pouring through the tear and flooding the engine rooms. It's traveling through the bottom of the ship. Sinking it."

"That's impossible." Karina scoffed. "The Titanic is unsinkable."

"The ocean is far more powerful than this ship," Mira said. "The Titanic is going to sink. At the rate the water is filling it up, I give it a few hours, tops."

"Can you stop it?" I asked.

"I can't fix the tear in the steel," she said. "The Titanic is going to sink, and there's nothing I can do about it."

"Then you have to come back with us," I said, but then I realized—Karina would be stuck here, because she couldn't go through the Eternal Library. She needed to be on solid land before I could return her to the present.

"I'm staying in 1912 with Karina, where Lilith can't reach me," Mira said. "There are lifeboats on board, and both of us are immune to the cold. We'll be okay until rescue comes for us."

"There aren't enough lifeboats," Karina said simply.

"Why wouldn't there be enough lifeboats?" I asked.

"White Star Line—the company that built the Titanic—called the ship 'unsinkable,'" she said. "More lifeboats would crowd up the Boat Deck. They removed some of the lifeboats so the first-class passengers could have more room to enjoy the outside space."

"Which means all of these people…" I looked around

at the third-class passengers, who were playing with chunks of ice like they had zero cares in the world.

"There aren't enough lifeboats for them all," Karina said. "First class passengers will be prioritized. As for the ones in steerage…" She looked around sadly, not continuing the sentence.

"They'll be left to go down with the ship," I said.

"Yes."

My heart ached for all of these doomed souls. So many of them were going to die because of what had happened here tonight.

Guilt filled me to the core, and I pushed it down to deal with later.

"So much for trying to create as little impact on the past as possible," I said. "If Time rejects the change, we'll lose the Dark Sword."

"As long as we don't directly affect one of the present-day Queens receiving her Object, Time is flexible," Mira said. "It will mold to the changes. And there's no Dark Queen of Swords yet. There's a good chance it will be okay."

"Hopefully," I said. "But I need *you* to be okay, too."

Karina straightened, determination filling her eyes. "Mira and I will be fine," she said. "I'll ensure she's properly dressed so she can take your place. As first-class passengers, we'll have a prime spot on the lifeboats. And if things get rough, I have my compulsion. We're going to be okay. Now, use that Queen of Pentacles magic of yours to get back home, bring the Dark Sword on Avalon, and help kill Lilith."

11

GEMMA

SUNDAY, APRIL 14, 1912

I USED my key to enter the Eternal Library, where Ethan was waiting for me in the ivory hall. He was alone—there was no sign of Hecate—and he was studying the Dark Sword.

It was made of obsidian, and there was a small red gemstone in the center of the handle. As I stepped closer, I felt the darkness pulsing off it. The red gem wasn't glowing, although I had a feeling it would once the Sword was in the hands of its rightful owner.

Relief crossed Ethan's face when he saw me. "I wanted to come after you," he said. "But I had a feeling you'd strangle me if I left the Sword unattended. Plus, I know Mira would never kill you."

"You thought right—on both accounts," I said, and

then I filled him in on everything that had happened on the ship after he'd left.

"So the Titanic's going to sink on her maiden voyage, without enough lifeboats, and with many well-known people on board," he said. "That will make history."

"*If* Time accepts the change," I said. "But still, all of those people will be dead."

"I know it's hard. But it's for the greater good," he said. "Otherwise, the demons could win the war and kill far more people than those who will go down with the ship."

"I know," I said, even though I still felt numb about it.

Deciding who would live and who would die was one of the most difficult parts of being a Queen. But it was my responsibility. And like Ethan had said, I believed I'd chosen the lesser of two evils. So I was going to make it worth it.

Which meant getting the Dark Sword to Avalon.

Hecate's realm blocked all magic but my witch magic, so Ethan and I had to go somewhere else before returning to the present. Going straight to Avalon to travel back to the present was out of the question, since in 1912 Avalon was a dead island with no doors, and I needed a door for Hecate's key to work.

"Where to?" I asked him.

"Hm." He scrunched his eyebrows as he thought,

since we had to go to a place we'd both been, that had existed in 1912. "Was Twin Pines Cafe around in this time?"

"No," I said. "They didn't build John Astor Road until later."

At the mention of the name of the street where I'd lived, my thoughts went to Madeline Astor. I hoped she and her husband had safely gotten on board a lifeboat.

Given what Karina had said about first class passengers being prioritized, I figured they had a much better chance than others.

"Then I guess the Haven tearoom," he said. "We just have to hope no one's in there when we enter."

"You might want to hide that." I motioned to the Dark Sword. "Just in case."

It was tough, but he managed to slide the Sword into the side of his pants and hide the handle with his jacket.

We used our keys to go to the Haven tearoom… and two people were in there. Mary and another vampire—one with doll-like features, long dark hair, and porcelain skin.

I immediately recognized her from her pictures in the history books.

Queen Laila. The vampire queen of the Vale before she'd been killed by Annika and replaced by King Alexander and Queen Deidre. She hardly looked dangerous—which I supposed was one of the scariest things about her.

Both she and Mary stared at us in shock.

"We're in the middle of a meeting," Mary said, and then she looked at us closer. "I thought I knew all of the citizens of the Haven. Have we met before?"

"Sorry—we were told that you were gone, and we came to clear the food," I said quickly, and then I scurried out of the room with Ethan, put the Holy Crown on my head, and brought us both back to the present.

"Sword still there?" I asked him when we reappeared in the hall.

If Time had rejected the change, it would be gone.

I held my breath as I waited for his answer.

He patted the side of his jacket. "Still here," he said, and he opened it slightly to show me.

Relief flooded my body.

Our mission had been a success.

At the same time, memories of the new timeline overlapped the ones of the original. Ethan's pupils dilated as the new memories filled his brain, too.

Like in the original timeline, Harper had sent us the fire message telling us to come to her room ASAP. But she hadn't needed to bring out a history book to give us information about the Titanic, since the ship was infamous for its tragic sinking on its maiden voyage. We already knew all about it, thanks to the award-winning movie.

Our mission in the new timeline had been to board the Titanic and find the Dark Sword before the ship sank. Karina had joined us both times, but in the new timeline, it was with the assumption that she'd easily get into one of the lifeboats and get picked up by the rescue ship—the Carpathia.

After getting the Dark Sword to Avalon, I was supposed to go to the port of New York City to grab Karina and take her home. But obviously, since she needed to look out for Mira back in 1912, that plan needed to change.

"We did it," I said with a huge smile, and I jumped into Ethan's arms and kissed him.

He swung me around in a circle and kissed me back.

Amidst all the chaos, I was so incredibly grateful that things were finally right between us.

"Ready to go back to Avalon?" he asked after placing me back down.

"Let's go," I said, and then I took out my key and stepped through the door.

12

GEMMA

TUESDAY, JUNE 1 (PRESENT DAY)

The Earth Angel—Annika Pearce, also known as the Queen of Cups—called a council meeting the moment we knocked on her door and showed her the Dark Sword.

The council met in the castle meeting room, around the ornate round table that had been used by King Arthur and his knights centuries ago. The council consisted of all four Queens, our chosen mates, and Skylar Danvers, the prophetess of Avalon.

The Dark Sword was laid out in the center of the table as we filled them in on everything that had happened in both the original timeline and this one.

"So Lilith is down two Queens," Annika said once we finished. "The Dark Queen of Swords can't be crowned, given that we're in possession of the Dark Sword, and

Mira is with Karina in 1912, where she's unreachable to everyone except for you."

"Correct," I said.

"Four Holy Queens against two Dark Queens," Raven said with a smirk. "We've got this."

"Except it's not that easy," Skylar said. "Unless you've forgotten about Lucifer?"

"Right." Raven huffed, sitting back in her chair and crossing her arms. "Him."

"Does anyone even know how to kill Lucifer?" Julian asked. "*Can* he be killed?"

"We don't know yet," Annika said softly. "But we're working on it."

One more question to add to my list of things to ask Hecate next time she showed up in the Library.

"Off-topic, but I have another question," Raven said, and she turned to look at me. "What on Earth's a 'pentacle?'"

I chuckled, since this wasn't the first time I'd gotten this question.

"It's a five-pointed star," I explained. "The five points of the star represent the five elements. Earth, air, water, fire, and spirit. Although in this case, spirit is my power as the Queen of Pentacles—time."

"Got it," she said, and then the double doors to the

council room were flung open, and Sage marched inside.

In her skin-tight black Avalon Army uniform, stiletto boots that had most likely been charmed by Bella to be comfortable no matter what, and her long dark hair streaming behind her, Sage looked like a force to be reckoned with.

Annika stood, immediately on guard. "You know you have high standing on Avalon," she said to Sage. "But council meetings are limited to council members only."

"It's calling to me." Sage sounded like she was in a trance. "It *needs* me."

We all watched her in shock as she reached over the table and grabbed the Dark Sword.

The gemstone in the center of the Sword glowed, and red magic swirled around the blade as it came to life. Sage's eyes gleamed red, too, and it was like her entire body was shining with magic.

She held the Dark Sword up high, relishing its power. After a few seconds, the red glow settled down, and she and the Sword were back to normal.

"The Dark Sword," Sage said, studying it with satisfaction. "It's *mine*."

Raven jumped to her feet, Excalibur held up in front of her, ready to fight. Noah stood at her side, his teeth bared, his fingers shifted into sharp claws.

"Whoa," Sage said, and she pointed the tip of the Dark Sword toward the floor. "I'm not going to hurt you."

"You're the Dark Queen of Swords." Raven's voice was calm and steady, although she watched Sage with shock and betrayal.

"I am," Sage said.

"But you're not dark."

"I'm a shifter," she said calmly. "Shifters were created by demons, just like Nephilim were created by angels. Dark magic runs in my blood."

"I know that," Raven said. "But *you're* not dark. You're not *evil*."

Sage remained still, as if she knew one wrong movement would set Raven off. "I've always had darkness in me—just like Noah and every other shifter has darkness in them," she said. "It doesn't make me evil. Just like how Bella Devereux isn't evil even though she practices dark magic."

"But now you're a dark *Queen*," Raven said. "It's different."

"I'm the exact same person you've known since I helped Noah save your life in that back alley in Santa Monica."

Raven lowered Excalibur slightly, although she didn't look fully convinced.

"Torrence uses dark magic," Selena pointed out. "She has control of it now, since Bella's been tutoring her. But the darkness doesn't consume her like it did when she got out of control. She's on our side. Just like Sage is."

Sage shot Selena a grateful smile. "Thanks for believing in me," she said.

"No problem."

Noah's claws shifted back to normal, which made me think he was coming around, too.

"This reminds me of something that Makena—one of the high witches of the Ward—told me and Mira while we were there," I said, and they all looked to me to continue. "She told me that other than the demons and angels, no one is purely good or purely evil. When guided by someone who believes in them, even the darkest souls have the potential to see the light."

"The Montgomery pack is drawn to darkness," Sage said. "My brother is a good enough example of that, given that he teamed up with demons. And I experienced a time of extreme darkness when I was bound to Azazel. But I kept hold of my true self the entire time. I may not have been able to physically fight the demon bond, but I never gave in mentally. That experience gave me the strength I need to fight with Avalon's army as the Dark Queen of Swords."

Raven studied Sage for a few more seconds, and then

she lowered Excalibur. "I suppose it's about time I had an equal partner to spar with," she said with a bit of friendly teasing in her tone.

"I can definitely manage that," Sage said lightly.

The two of them shared a smile, and I could tell that things were already back to normal between them.

It reminded me of me and Mira when we forgave each other after a fight. We didn't need to say anything—it was just *known* that everything was okay again. Just like it had been on the deck of the Titanic after she'd thrown her magic at the ocean instead of at me.

Raven and Sage might not be twins, but they were best friends, and that connection counted for something, too.

"The two of you will have to save your sparring session for later," Annika said, and then she looked to Sage and continued, "I need you to find Thomas and bring him here. Because the two of you are the newest members of Avalon's council, and we need all council members here to continue with this meeting."

13

GEMMA

TUESDAY, JUNE 1 (PRESENT DAY)

A FEW HOURS LATER, Thomas and Sage were sitting around the round table, fully briefed on everything that had been going on.

"So, Lilith needs the gifted vampire blood to raise Lucifer," Sage said.

"Correct," I replied.

"And what will happen after Lucifer is released from his prison realm?"

"In the Bible, Lilith is regarded as secretive and conniving," Skylar said, and we all looked to her to continue. "She's snake-like and is often associated with the serpent in the Garden of Eden."

"It explains the snake-like way that she and Lavinia worked together to trick Mira into that demon bond," I said.

"It also explains why she's been leading her side of the war from the shadows," Skylar said. "Lucifer, on the other hand, isn't known for being inconspicuous. Once he's released, he'll likely want us all to know it."

"How do you know all of this?" Ethan asked.

"When I was human, I owned a new age shop," she said. "I immersed myself in the study of all kinds of mysticism."

"'Immersed' is an understatement," Raven said, rolling her eyes. "She was obsessed. *Is* obsessed."

"That's what happens when a person has a higher calling," Skylar said, and then she turned back to Sage. "I take it you had a reason for asking?"

"I did." Sage sat straighter, her eyes taking on a look of hard determination. "As always, we can't find Lilith. Which means we need to get her to come out in the open. Mira told Gemma that as the Dark Queen of Cups, Lilith will lead the ceremony to raise Lucifer. Does anyone have any idea where the Hell Gate to his prison realm is located?"

She looked around at everyone at the table, but no one had any answers.

"I might be able to find someone who does," I said, and then I stood up, walked across the room, stuck my key in the door, and stepped into the ivory hall of the Eternal Library.

Hecate stood across the hall, waiting for me. She wore a purple gown that sparkled with what looked like nighttime stars, and her dark hair glimmered like it was shining under the moonlight.

"Gemma," she greeted me. "You've had quite the adventure since the last time we met."

"You mean how I witnessed one of the most famous maritime disasters in all of history?" I asked.

"I assume that isn't the question you came here to ask."

"No," I said, cursing inwardly at myself for my careless phrasing. "Of course not."

"I figured as much." She gave me a knowing smile, then led me into the endless hall of books, and I asked her my *real* question.

14

GEMMA

TUESDAY, JUNE 1 (PRESENT DAY)

I RE-ENTERED Avalon's meeting room with a triumphant smile.

"She was there?" Ethan asked, but he must have already known my answer, because he jumped up, used his key, and walked through the door.

He came back a few seconds later, looking bummed.

"Was she gone?" I asked.

"Yep."

"Interesting." This was the first time Ethan and I had ever entered the Eternal Library alone. It had never crossed my mind that Hecate would be there for me and then no-show for Ethan on the same day.

"Where did you go?" Annika asked us.

"I needed to double check something," I said simply, and then Ethan and I returned to our seats around the round table without any further questions. "I know the location of the Lucifer's Hell Gate."

"Why didn't you say something earlier?" Raven asked.

"I didn't want to say anything until I knew for sure."

She nodded, apparently accepting my explanation.

"So?" Selena sat forward, impatient. "Where is it?"

"Las Vegas," I said. "Right in the center of the Vegas Strip."

"Vegas," Sage said with a small chuckle. "Very fitting."

The others nodded, and some of them smiled slightly. It was hard to miss the irony of the situation.

"She probably has demons and dark witches stationed there," Raven said. "I could go with the Nephilim army and start clearing them out."

"And alert Lilith that we know the location of Lucifer's Hell Gate?" Julian said, his tone making it clear that he thought that was a terrible idea. "We need a better strategy than that."

"Agreed," said Thomas. "We shouldn't make our presence known. But we can spy on them without them knowing we're there."

"How?" Selena asked.

"There are cameras in every casino in Vegas," he said. "They're called the Eyes in the Sky."

"You can hack into them," Annika realized. "We can do surveillance from right here on Avalon."

Of course. Thomas was a gifted vampire—his gift was with technology. I wasn't quite sure how it worked, but he could definitely use his gift to tune into the cameras in Vegas.

"I can go there pretty discreetly," he said. "There are supernatural groups of all kinds living in Vegas. Vampires, shifters, witches. All I need to do is touch the walls of the buildings, and we're in."

"And we can talk to the supernaturals who already live there," Raven said. "Get them to keep lookout for us, too."

"This circles back to my original idea," Sage said. "Because eventually, Lilith will go to Vegas to raise Lucifer. Once we get word that she's there, we'll teleport in, ready to strike."

"But she may never go there to raise him," I pointed out. "Remember what Mira said—Lilith needs enough fresh gifted vampire blood to soak the ground around the Hell Gate."

"Our army has been finding the bunkers where the demons are keeping the gifted humans and rescuing them," Raven said proudly. "Saving the gifted humans before she can turn them into vampires is how we've held her off from raising Lucifer for this long."

"And it's working," Sage said. "Maybe too well."

"What do you mean?"

"I mean that we need Lilith in Vegas, ready to raise Lucifer. She can't go there unless she has enough gifted vampire blood to do the spell."

"What are you saying?" I asked, even though I had a pretty good idea of what she was saying.

I just needed her to say it out loud, to be sure.

"I'm saying that we stop rescuing the gifted humans from the bunkers," Sage said. "We let her turn them into vampires, so she has enough gifted vampire blood to go to Vegas and perform the spell."

Horror splashed across Annika's face. "You want us to sacrifice all those innocent people," she said.

"It's been over fifteen years, and we're no closer to finding Lilith than we were back then," Sage said. "This is war. In war, sacrifices need to be made."

"These are innocent people," argued Annika.

"The longer we let this war continue, the more people will be killed," Sage said. "By getting Lilith to Vegas, we can end it sooner than later."

She looked around the table, sizing up who might take her side.

I instantly thought of my time in Ember—when the dragon had sacrificed himself to give us his heart to track the Holy Crown.

But that had been different.

He'd been willing.

These humans would be casualties that could have been saved.

But for how long? The Nephilim army was able to find some of the bunkers and save the gifted humans there, but not all of them. Humans were dying anyway—it was just taking longer than it would have otherwise. Why extend this war when we could kill Lilith before she raised Lucifer and put an end to this once and for all?

"We need to talk about this further," Annika said. "And then we'll do what this council is here for—we'll take a vote."

15

GEMMA

THURSDAY, JUNE 24 (PRESENT DAY)

For the past three weeks, we'd been doing the only thing useful to do in a time like this—preparing for the battle to come.

Because it *would* be coming.

Soon.

Ethan and I were on one of the training grounds when Annika teleported in.

"It's time," she said, and then she took both of us to the council room, where the others were waiting.

They jumped into it immediately once we got there.

"I've alerted the Nephilim army and the witches that it's about to happen," Raven said. "They're waiting for the fire message, and then they'll head out."

"The supernaturals in Vegas have been notified, too," Thomas said.

Sage held tightly onto the Dark Sword. "I can't wait to give Lilith what's coming to her," she said, and then she ran her finger along the flat side of the Sword, like she was petting it. "I'm glad this thing lets me kill greater demons, despite the fact that I'm not Nephilim."

"If I get to her first, I'm taking her down," Raven said. "She's either of ours to kill."

"Then it's a race to see who gets to her first," Sage said, and they shared a friendly, competitive smile.

Annika cleared her throat, and all eyes were on her. "I'd give an encouraging speech on how we've been preparing for this for years, but Lilith isn't going to wait to raise Lucifer," she said, and then she sat down at the table. "Bring me a pen and paper, and I'll get the message to our army."

16

GEMMA

THURSDAY, JUNE 24 (PRESENT DAY)

There was only one adult on Avalon who couldn't leave the island—Annika.

When she'd first arrived on Avalon and the island was dead, she'd used her magic as the Earth Angel to sign a contract with the island to bring it back to life. It was a contract signed with her blood, which meant her life force was what was keeping Avalon alive.

If she left Avalon, the island would die.

Eventually, the only people left on the island were me, Ethan, Annika, Bella, Torrence, the children who were too young to fight, and the full fae, since their iron allergy made it impossible for them to go to Earth.

Annika looked at me, her golden eyes as serious as ever. "You know your job," she said.

"Yes," I replied. "I know."

Remain at the vantage point.
Observe the battle.
Stay alive.

If we lost, and if I died, then that would be it. There'd be no second chances.

I owed it to the world to remain in the shadows, and to stay alive. That was one of the main things I'd learned from the beginning of my reign as Queen as Pentacles— I was an observer of time, destined to mold it in the shadows. Most would never know how large of a role I played in shaping the future.

I was at peace with that. I'd come to peace with it when I'd returned from saving Selena's life.

"Then go," Annika said. "And return to me with news that we've won this war, once and for all."

Torrence stepped up to stand in front of me, and Bella did the same with Ethan.

"I'll keep you safe," Ethan promised me. "Always."

"I know," I said, and we shared a loving smile.

Then he took Bella's hands, I took Torrence's, and they teleported us out.

We reappeared on the open-air roof of the Stratosphere —the hotel at the end of the Las Vegas Strip with an observation tower that looked out over the wide street. It was the second tallest observation tower in the Western Hemisphere, which made it the perfect spot for the job I needed to do.

There were a few thrill rides at the top of it, and tourists were enjoying themselves on them without a care in the world.

Humans who could likely become casualties in this battle.

Unfortunately, there was nothing we could do to clear them out without alerting Lilith and her dark army that we knew they were coming. It was another one of those hard decisions—we were putting a fraction of people at risk to save the world.

I hated it.

But it was what needed to be done.

I stared down the street full of massive hotels that was lit by the bright Vegas sun. Lilith had likely chosen to do this during the day on purpose—it made it so the vampires in Avalon's Army had to either stay inside the hotels or be weakened if they went out in the sun. But we had enough Nephilim, witches, and shifters on our side to hold our ground.

She'd also likely chosen this particular day on purpose. Because the normally traffic-packed Strip was devoid of cars. There was a marathon run tonight—it was called Running with the Devil—so the road was cleared to provide safety for the runners.

Besides that, everything on the Strip looked normal. But that was because supernaturals were good at blending in. Thanks to Thomas's ability to magically hack into the camera systems, we knew Lilith's dark witches had been teleporting demons into the hotels all morning.

Which was why our people were stationed on the sidewalks along the street, wearing cloaking crystals to hide themselves from the dark army. Thanks to my supernaturally strong vision, I was able to see a few of the witches and shifters I knew from Avalon.

The people who'd be more recognizable to the dark army—the other Queens and major players—were in the shadows, waiting to emerge when the time came.

"Are you scared?" Ethan asked, bringing me back to the present.

I looked at him, then back at the packed Strip. "Not as scared as I should be."

"Because we're going to win," Torrence said with a confident smirk. "We always do."

"Not always," Bella said, and it was true—Avalon's Army had lost fights with demons over the years. "But we hold our own when it matters most."

"We do," I agreed. "But being a time traveler is

strange sometimes. Since I can go back in time and change the present, the present doesn't feel as immediate to me as it did before I became the Queen of Pentacles. It feels more like a dress rehearsal than real life."

"Which is why we're here on this tower," Ethan said. "To analyze the 'dress rehearsal' so we're ready if a second performance is necessary."

"It won't be," Torrence said. "But it's good to know you have our backs, just in case."

"I always have your backs," I promised, and then I heard a strange, soft whirring sound in the distance. I looked out to where it was coming from and saw a pack of black dots rise over the mountains and fly toward us.

Helicopters.

Tons of them.

Horror pooled within me as they reached the Strip, the sounds of their blades growing so loud that it infiltrated my brain. Tourists stopped walking and gazed up, using their hands as visors to block the sun.

The helicopters got lower, and it was obvious that they weren't normal helicopters. Each of them had the outline of a circle around the bottom of it. And on the undersides were what looked like faucets.

"Why are there crop-dusters flying over the Strip?" a tourist asked nearby.

"They're probably gonna make it rain!" his friend said loudly—he sounded drunk. "I hope it's vodka in there!"

Despite the heat, I shivered.

Because there was no way those things were carrying vodka.

"Blood," I whispered to Ethan. "Lilith's going to make it rain gifted vampire blood."

As I said it, the red liquid started spraying out of the bottoms of the helicopters. A giant cloud of red formed above the Strip as the blood rained down from one helicopter, and then the next, and then the next. The blood was so thick that it was impossible to see anything.

It was like a scene from a horror movie.

Screams filled the air.

"Torrence and I need to get a closer look at what's happening," Bella said. "The two of you—stay here."

They were gone before we could reply.

I reached for Ethan's hand and squeezed it. The helicopters were focusing on the center of the Strip, so there wasn't any blood at the top of the Stratosphere, but its metallic scent filled my nose and mouth.

The screams intensified—an eerie chorus echoing out of the red storm.

Bella reappeared next to us. She was covered in blood—her skin looked like it had been dyed red—and blood dripped from her hair. "Our shifters have changed into their animal forms and they're scaring the humans to get them inside the hotels," she said. "They're not hurting the humans, but there are demons and dark witches down there, too. They've already started to fight, but our people are holding them off."

"Where's Torrence?" I asked.

"She stayed down there to help."

Of course she did. Torrence wasn't one to stay on the sidelines.

We stood there for what must have been thirty minutes, watching helicopter after helicopter fly over the Strip and spray blood over the street.

Blue lightning flashed inside the ominous red cloud—Selena's magic.

Bella popped in and out, giving us reports of what was going on down there.

Most of the humans had gone inside and were hiding out in the hotels. Avalon's army was fighting the dark army, and luckily for the humans, the dark army only cared about killing supernaturals. And, according to Bella, our army was slaughtering the dark one.

Maybe I wouldn't have to go back in time for a redo, after all.

Finally, the last helicopters finished raining blood upon the Strip, and the air started to clear.

Bodies were strewn across the pavement. Most of them didn't appear to be anyone I recognized. There were also piles of ashes everywhere.

The remains of demons.

Avalon's army had killed so many of them. And our army was standing strong. Selena, Raven, and Sage stood shoulder-to-shoulder, with Selena in the center, radiating magic out of the Holy Wand. Nephilim, witches, and shifters that I recognized were behind them, weapons drawn and ready to fight. They were all drenched in blood, and they looked terrifying.

They stared up at the helicopters, wind blowing all around as the vehicles lowered themselves down so they were hovering about fifty feet above the street. The helicopters flew in a circle, with the largest one in the center.

A blinding flash of red light exploded from the central helicopter—so bright and painful that I had to hold my hand in front of my eyes and turn around. It was like the entire world was red. Not even closing my eyes or holding my hand in front of my face could stop me from seeing it.

Finally the light died down, and I turned back around.

The central helicopter had landed… and it sat in the middle of a large, red barrier dome.

Selena shot blue lightning out of the Holy Wand toward the dome, but the lightning simply spread out along it and fizzled out. She tried again, and again, with the same results each time.

Raven and Sage tried to wham the dome with their Swords, but they were unsuccessful as well.

The three of them stopped launching their attacks when four women wearing long white robes stepped out of the helicopter, all of them with jet-black hair and pale white skin. I assumed they were Foster witches.

Lavinia followed them. She held the Dark Wand, its red crystals glowing like spotlights next to her.

Next out was a woman with long, flowing hair, and hard, cat-like features. She wore leather pants, a black corset top, and she was holding a metallic, charcoal-gray chalice with both of her hands.

Lilith.

And she was carrying the Dark Grail.

17

RAVEN

THURSDAY, JUNE 24 (PRESENT DAY)

My grip around the Holy Sword tightened the moment Lilith stepped out of that helicopter, and my blood boiled at the sight of her.

I'd been hunting her for over sixteen years.

And now, it was time to take her down.

I ran forward and smashed its blade into the red boundary dome, putting all the force into the blow that I could muster.

Pain seared through me, like I'd been electrocuted. Still, that didn't stop me from trying again, and again, until every nerve in my body felt like it had been fried to oblivion.

"Raven!" someone called from behind me. Noah. He wrapped his arms around me—he must have shifted back into human form and some point—and he pulled me away from the dome. "It isn't working. You're hurting yourself each time you try."

He was right. I knew it.

But it didn't mean I liked it.

"If I have to hurt myself to get to her, then so be it," I said, although I didn't fight to escape his hold on me.

Lavinia smiled devilishly, and the red crystal on the Dark Wand hummed. "You can't break through my barrier," she said.

"Maybe she can't," Sage said from behind me. "But I can."

She ran forward, raised the Dark Sword in the air, and smashed it against the barrier dome that surrounded Lilith, Lavinia, and the Foster witches.

Red electricity burst out of Sage's sword and crackled over the dome, the light so bright that it was nearly blinding. I had no choice but to turn away from it. Once the light died down, I inhaled the charred air and looked to see what had happened.

The barrier dome was gone.

Sage had fallen down to the ground, the Dark Sword in her hand. She sat up, frazzled, but alive.

Thomas zipped to her side, despite the fact that the vampires were supposed to stay out of the sun unless absolutely necessary, and checked to see if she was okay.

Lavinia's lips curled upward, and she pointed the

Dark Wand at Sage. "Finally—the Dark Queen of Swords is revealed," she said. "Come, take your place at our side, where you belong."

"I belong with Avalon," she said, and she stood up, ready to fight.

Lavinia changed the angle of the Dark Wand and shot a red beam of light at Thomas.

I ran forward to use my Sword to stop its magic, but Sage was quicker. The red light bounced off her blade, saving Thomas's life. Then Selena was there, and her blue magic collided with Lavinia's red magic, a loud crack filling the air as the beams of light met in the space between them.

Selena's blue magic inched toward Lavinia's red, and Lavinia's eyes narrowed as she fought against her. But Selena was more powerful than Lavinia. She had this.

And, now that I knew my friends were still alive, I turned my focus back to Lilith—just in time to see her turn the Dark Grail upside down and let a thick, oily liquid cascade to the ground.

Its metallic scent was unmistakable—blood. Dark, black, unnatural blood.

It sizzled as it hit the pavement, and horror filled me to the bones.

"*Now*, He will rise," Lilith said, and her eyes flashed

red as the black blood crawled over the pavement, forming a sort of sinkhole as it spread out.

Lavinia moved to Lilith's side—she and Selena must have stopped fighting when Lilith dumped the contents of the Dark Grail to the ground.

Finally, the pit stopped growing, and black mist that reminded me of Torrence's dark mage magic rose out of it like steam. The pit reeked of death—like a million demons had been rotting inside of it for centuries. A knot of fear formed in my throat, and I couldn't swallow it down.

Because I knew what was in that pit. *Who* was in that pit.

Lucifer.

But the things that emerged from it weren't shaped like a human. They were dogs. Big, black dogs with eyes that glowed demonic red.

"Hellhounds," Noah whispered from next to me, his voice laced with fear.

He barely had a chance to finish saying the word before I surged forward, dancing around the Hellhounds and swinging the Holy Sword through the air. I sliced off their heads and speared them through their hearts, turning them into piles of ashes around me. I caught a glimpse of Sage in the corner of my eye, and she was doing the same. Selena worked with us, too, using the tip of the Holy Wand as a sword as she rammed it through their hearts to slay them.

I was out of breath by the time all the Hellhounds were dead.

None of them had gotten past us.

I smiled as I looked out toward the Stratosphere hotel, where Gemma stood on the roof with Ethan, watching us win this battle.

But my attention quickly refocused on the pit—because something else was rising out of it. A tall, broad, muscular, naked man. He was four times as big as a human, and his presence made the air thrum with dark, heavy magic. His nails were long, black claws that protruded out of his fingers like ten swords, and I gripped Excalibur tighter at the sight of them.

Once he was fully out of the pit, the ground stitched itself together beneath his feet.

Lilith, Lavinia, and the dark witches gazed up at him, looking as intimidated by his presence as I felt.

But Lilith straightened and held the Dark Grail closer to her chest. "Kill them," she commanded, and Lucifer smirked, like he'd been thinking the same thing.

I ran forward, Sword held high in the air, took a large, leaping jump, and aimed the tip of it at his heart.

The Sword collided with his skin with a crash, but it

didn't break through—just like it hadn't broken through Lavinia's barrier dome.

Every bone in my body felt like it shattered on impact. My ears buzzed so loudly that I couldn't hear. It was like someone had struck a gong inside my head, and it wasn't shutting off.

The next thing I knew, I was lying on the ground, Lucifer's claws slashed at my throat, and everything went dark.

18

SELENA

THURSDAY, JUNE 24 (PRESENT DAY)

I FROZE and stared at Raven's body in shock—at the blood gushing out of the place where her neck used to connect to her head. Her head had been disconnected from her body. Her golden-rimmed eyes sightlessly gazed up at the darkened sky, and her skin was paler than ever.

The Holy Sword lay next to her, no longer in her grip.

She was dead.

Raven was *dead.*

It didn't feel real. Because Raven was the Queen of Swords. She was unstoppable. The best fighter around.

But Lucifer had slain her in a single swipe.

If she couldn't kill him, then who could?

The thoughts flashed through my mind in what must

have been less than a second. The next thing I knew, a beam of red light shot toward me, and Julian pushed me out of the way before it hit.

"Use the Wand against Lucifer," he said, and then he hopped over Raven's body and picked up Excalibur. He moved in a flash to stand back beside me, and when Lavinia aimed another beam of red magic at me, he used the Holy Sword to reflect it back at Lucifer.

But the demon king simply stood there, *absorbing* the red magic as if it were energy soaking into his body. He even gave Julian what I thought was a challenging smile. As if asking him to bring it on.

I raised the Holy Wand, gathered as much magic as I could, and shot a blue beam of magic out of the crystal at the top.

Lucifer simply stood there, absorbing my magic, too. You wouldn't have even known we were attacking if you didn't see the red and blue laser beams hitting his chest.

Frustration surged through me, and the sky rolled with thunder as I called on the magic gifted to me by the god Jupiter. I gathered more magic than ever before, connected with the dark cloud that had formed above us, and struck Lucifer with a dozen bolts of lightning at once.

I expected a pile of ash to remain in the spot where Lucifer had stood.

But he was still there.

He wasn't even charred. He was just standing there, watching us like we were bugs entertaining him as he waited to squash us.

Not possible.

Lilith cackled from her spot behind Lucifer. "You're unprepared to fight him," she said. "There's nothing you can do that will work. You might as well give up now."

I glanced at Julian, who was still using Excalibur against Lavinia's magic. Sweat poured down his face, his cheeks red with exertion. The Sword hadn't chosen him like it had chosen Raven—Julian wasn't the King of Swords. But he was still able to wield Excalibur. Not as easily as Raven, but he could do it.

"I'm going to need you to keep holding her off," he said, low enough that only I could hear him. Then he glanced behind us, where the others stood in a line, ready to fight. "Sage," he called, and the Dark Queen of Swords flashed to our side. "Let's use both Swords on him at once."

"No," I said. "You saw what happened to Raven." My eyes drifted to where Raven lay on the street in a puddle of her blood. Now someone else lay dead next to her—Noah. There was a bleeding hole in his heart, and one of his arms wrapped around Raven, protecting her even in death.

Sickness rose into my throat, and I forced myself to look away.

"Do you have any better ideas?" Julian asked.

We can leave, I thought, but I didn't say it out loud. Because we were the best bet to kill Lucifer.

We had to try.

Suddenly, the Nephilim were running around us, leaping forward and aiming their holy weapons at Lucifer just like Raven had done.

Just like what had happened to Raven, their weapons did nothing against the demon king. They bounced off him, and the Nephilim fell to the ground one after the other.

Lucifer used his claws to shred them to pieces.

Lavinia aimed the Dark Wand's red magic at the rest of them, frying them one by one.

"Stop!" I screamed, but my voice was drowned out in the chaos.

Before I knew what was happening, Julian and Sage ran toward Lucifer and did exactly what Julian had planned—hit Lucifer's chest with the Holy Sword and the Dark Sword at the same time.

It was no more effective than anything else.

Their bodies slammed to the ground, Lucifer raised his claws to kill them, and then every cell in my body exploded in a red flash of light.

19

GEMMA

THURSDAY, JUNE 24 (PRESENT DAY)

Lavinia's magic surrounded Selena in a bright ball of red. She aimed more and more of it at where Selena had been standing, and I held my breath, waiting for Selena's blue magic to emerge—waiting for a sign that she was still alive.

Nothing happened.

Finally, Lavinia let go of her magic.

Charred remains were in the place where Selena had been standing, so twisted that they barely looked human.

Jacen—her father—ran to her side, then was quickly obliterated by Lavinia's magic, too.

Torrence and Reed ran forward, throwing their black, smoky dark mage magic at Lavinia. The two of them together were holding her off—but barely.

Lucifer continued to simply stand there, like the entire bloodbath amused him.

"We have to go back," I said to Ethan. "We have to fix this."

"None of their weapons are working against Lucifer," he said, and his eyes flashed with determination. "Stay here. I'll be back in a minute."

Before I could ask him what he was doing, he exploded into dragon form and soared through the sky until he hovered over Lucifer. He pulled his neck back, then released a blast of fire at the demon king.

Terror swirled inside me.

No.

If Selena's lightning hadn't worked against Lucifer, then why would Ethan's fire do anything different?

I held my breath, watching as he continued aiming his fire at Lucifer.

I was a second away from screaming at him to come back when a sword soared through the sky, heading straight toward him.

The Dark Sword.

It pierced Ethan's chest, and my heart shattered in mine, too.

His neck arched up, a final stream of fire burst from his mouth, and my soul felt like it split from my body as I watched him fall to the ground. The moment he hit the pavement, he returned to his human form.

Dead.

It felt like a fist wrapped itself around my heart, squeezing so much that I couldn't breathe. My chest hurt. *Everything* hurt. The emptiness was all consuming, and all I could do was stand there, frozen, like time had stopped in place.

This couldn't be happening.

This couldn't be real.

But somehow, I caught my breath and collected myself. Because this was just a dress rehearsal.

I'd seen everything I needed to see. And I wasn't going to let this timeline solidify.

I was going to change it.

So I ran to the door that led inside the Stratosphere, put my key in the lock, and stepped inside the ivory hall of Hecate's Eternal Library.

The goddess of witchcraft waited inside, her dark hair draped in waves around her shoulders. "Gemma," she said calmly. "I expected you'd come."

"Nothing they did killed Lucifer." My voice sounded dull and flat to my ears. "They couldn't kill him. They couldn't even hurt him. *Nothing* worked. Not the Holy Sword, or the Holy Wand… and not Ethan's fire." My throat closed up when I said his name.

"There's only one way to kill Lucifer," Hecate said.

I stared at her, amazed that she'd given me information without me asking a question.

She was trying to help me. She wanted me to ask the *right* question. More than that—she'd basically just told me the question I should ask.

"How can we kill Lucifer?" I stared at her, waiting, desperate for an answer.

"I was hoping you'd ask." Her violet eyes shimmered with approval. "Come with me, and I'll tell you." She led the way into the never-ending hall of books and took her place at the pedestal in front. Then she released the smokey mist from her eyes, letting it crawl through the shelves to search for the information she needed.

It didn't take long for a book to fly out—a book so black it looked like a dark hole that led into the ether.

It was the same deep black as the pit Lilith had opened to release Lucifer.

The book settled onto the pedestal and opened to a page near the end.

Hecate barely glanced at the writing inside. "There's only one weapon that can kill Lucifer," she said, her eyes locked on mine. "The Golden Scepter that was once wielded by the Angel of Death. As the most powerful weapon in the world, it can only be wielded by an angel."

"But we can't access the realm of the angels," I said.

"No," she said. "But there's an angel who lives on Earth."

"Annika."

"Yes." Hecate nodded.

Except Annika couldn't leave Avalon. But that was a problem for later. Right now, there was something more important I needed to know.

"Where can I find the Golden Scepter?"

"I've already answered your question of the day," she said. "I'm sorry. That's all the information I can give you."

"I can come back tomorrow," I begged, tears forming in my eyes. "Meet me here tomorrow. Please."

"You have the resources to do the rest of this on your own," she said. "You have strong magic. Use it. Tune into it. Believe in yourself. You can do this."

I wanted to beg her to tell me more. I wanted to tell her that I'd do *anything* for her to give me any bit of information that could help me locate the Scepter.

But I'd been to the Eternal Library enough to know when Hecate was done for the day.

And deep inside myself, I knew she wouldn't leave me with nothing to go on.

So I swallowed down my tears and looked Hecate straight in the eyes. "I *will* do this," I said, and then I hurried into the ivory hall, used my key to unlock the door, and stepped back onto Avalon.

20

MIRA

THURSDAY, APRIL 18, 1912

I'D ALWAYS WANTED to see New York City.

But I never dreamed I'd be seeing it in the year 1912.

The past hour had been a whirlwind. The Carpathia—the ship that had rescued us while we were in the lifeboats after the Titanic sank—had docked at the Port of New York. A huge crowd had gathered to greet the survivors, and Karina and I had pushed through it, quickly getting lost in it.

The first thing Karina had done was bring us to a dress shop, since all we'd had on us when the ship sank were our nightclothes. Now, we were making our way down the sidewalk toward the Upper East Side. The new dress was big and uncomfortable, but wearing it made me feel like I was living in a fantasy world instead of real life. The cars that drove down the streets were all buggies, and instead of modern skyscrapers, the buildings were made of detailed stone and marble. It was so surreal—like we'd been plopped into a movie set.

"We'll stay in the St. Regis hotel," Karina said. "The best hotel in the city."

"And how are we going to afford that?" I had no money on me, and neither did Karina. Everything we'd brought with us onto the Titanic had been lost when the ship sank. "You can't compel an entire company to give us a hotel room like you can compel a dress maker to give us clothing."

"Easy," Karina said, and she hurried over to a well-dressed man walking ahead of us. "Excuse me," she said, and the man stopped to listen to her. When she continued speaking, her voice had a musical quality to it—she was using compulsion. "You're going to give me all of the money you have on you. Then you're going to continue on your way and forget this ever happened."

His eyes glazed over, he removed his wallet from his jacket pocket, took out all the cash, and handed it to Karina. "Have a good day," he said, and he tilted his hat to her, then to me, and continued on his way.

Karina counted the money, turned to me, then flashed me a dangerous grin. "You see?" she said as she put the cash into her pocket. "Easy."

She continued on her way, and I followed in a daze.

Because it had been a crazy few days on the Carpathia as Karina had helped clarify everything Gemma had told me about Ethan.

My memories of Ethan weren't real.

I didn't want to believe it, but I knew in my heart it was true. Because ever since the day we'd gotten our magic, I'd known every time Ethan looked at me that he wasn't the same as before. I'd known something had changed.

Now, I knew what that something was.

Ethan had never loved me.

He'd always loved Gemma.

They were twin flames, and I had no one.

Now, in this new city in a strange time, I felt more alone than ever. But at least I had Karina. Without her, I would have been completely lost.

Karina held her head proudly as she walked past the men in suits in front of the hotel, and I followed her through the revolving doors.

Once inside, I stopped and gazed around in awe at what was definitely the fanciest hotel I'd ever been in. The floors were marble, columns lined the walls, and a crystal chandelier hung in the entrance.

Karina marched up to the desk, and the man working behind it looked up at us.

"My sister and I need a suite," Karina said, using

compulsion again. "We'll be staying for an extended amount of time, so book no one else in our room until we leave."

He told us the nightly price, and Karina counted out the bills and handed them over to him.

"We'll pay on a weekly basis," she said, and of course, he agreed. Then he grabbed two keys from behind the desk—two *real* keys, not those plastic cards they use in present-day hotels—and handed them to us. "Is your luggage waiting outside?"

"No luggage," Karina said, and he nodded, as if this was totally normal.

He called for a butler, and the butler led us into the elevator and showed us to the room. He made a huge deal out of explaining everything about the suite, informed us that we could leave our shoes outside our door each night so they could be shined, then saw himself out.

I walked over to one of the windows and looked out at the people walking along the street below.

In New York City.

In *1912*.

This was crazy.

Finally, I looked back over at Karina. "What are we going to do while we're here?" I asked her.

"As much as I dislike it, we're going to have to live

quietly," she said. "Make as few waves in time as possible."

"So we're going to stay in the hotel room?"

"We'll limit our interactions with others, but we'll have to leave to get money," she said. "And food. And fresh air. Before the time of air conditioning, buildings were too stuffy to stay indoors all the time." She shuddered, as if the thought of remaining indoors horrified her.

As someone who loved being outside, staying indoors all the time horrified me, too.

"How long will we have to stay here?" I asked, trying to ignore the part of me that never wanted to leave.

Because if I stayed here, I wouldn't have to face everything that waited for me back home.

I'd never have to look into Ethan's eyes and be reminded that he'd never loved me. That my memories of the two of us together were a lie.

I'd never have to see my sister and be reminded of her betrayal. Because at the end of the day, she knew she had feelings for Ethan, and she'd kept her feelings secret from me.

Can you blame her? I thought. *Would you tell her if the situation was reversed?*

I wished I could say I would, but the truth was, I wasn't sure.

"We stay until Lilith is dead," Karina said. "You said you'd know when the bond is severed."

"I will," I said, since the bond was like a thin blanket wrapped around me. Here in the past, I wasn't bound by it. In the present, it controlled my every move.

"Good," she said. "Now, let's get going. There's a lovely bar downstairs, and I need something to drink."

21

MIRA

SUNDAY, APRIL 28, 1912

AFTER ONE WEEK of living in New York City in 1912, I found I didn't hate it as much as anticipated. The dresses were a pain, but the distance from Lilith's hold—and the distance from Ethan—were helping me fight the darkness that had haunted my soul since watching Ethan place the Holy Crown on Gemma's head.

Karina and I spent a decent amount of time at restaurants, where we kept to ourselves. Today, we were on a stroll through Central Park. The sky was covered with clouds, which meant the sun didn't weaken Karina like it would on a bright day. Plus, with the gowns and hats of the era, she was able to cover herself enough that we could go out during normal hours.

In the park, spring was in full bloom, with new leaves on the trees and flowers on the grass. It was strange to feel immersed in nature in the middle of a city. Karina even walked me to a spot in the park where no buildings were visible at all.

Eventually, she zeroed in on the reason we were there—to find a wealthy man she could compel for money. She'd already selected the one she wanted—a young bachelor named William Bradshaw who was one of the wealthiest men in the city. He was the proud owner of one of the world's first compact cameras, and could often be found taking photos on Sunday afternoons in the park. This was a hot topic of gossip amongst the single women in the city, who purposefully timed their afternoon strolls so they could walk past him and try to catch his eye.

He was easy to spot—a man a few years older than me, kneeling to capture a photo of bluebirds on a fountain. His sandy blond hair blew in the wind, and he didn't seem to mind that he might mess up his trousers —probably because he could easily purchase new ones.

When Karina had first told me about him, I'd assumed he'd be high-brow and stuffy, like most of the wealthy men in New York. Instead, he struck me as carefree, artsy, and sensitive.

Not usually my type... but something drew me toward him.

I wanted to know him.

"Pick someone else," I said to Karina, and then I reached for my air magic and created a strong enough wind to blow my hat off my head and straight into the lens of William's camera.

I ran after it, as if I needed to chase the wind, and watched him catch the hat and look around for its owner.

He sucked in a sharp breath when his brown eyes met mine, and I froze in place.

He was one of the most handsome men I'd ever seen.

The corner of his lip curled up in amusement, and he held the hat out to me. "I take it this is yours?" he asked.

"Yes." I reached forward to take it from him, and when my fingers brushed his, warmth flooded from my hand to my heart. "Thank you for rescuing it for me."

He tilted his head and watched me with interest, still not letting go of the hat. "Where are you from?" he asked.

Right—the accent.

There weren't many Australians around here. Even so, my accent was different from theirs, given that over a century had passed between this time and mine.

"Australia," I said, and his eyes widened with interest.

"I've always dreamed of going to Australia," he said. "Taking photos of the wildlife and of the cliffs in the south. I've heard that not even photographs can do its beauty justice, but I'd try my hardest anyway."

"I'm from the south of Melbourne, and I agree—nothing compares to actually standing on the coves that line our beaches," I said, but then I quickly realized that I should have thought before speaking. Because was Melbourne even a city back in 1912?

I should know more about the place where I lived, but I'd never been much of a history buff.

"Fascinating," he said, although from the way he was watching me, it seemed like he found me far more fascinating than my home country. "What brings you to New York?"

I glanced at the hat, which we were still holding between us, and he grinned sheepishly as he released it to me.

"I was spending some time with my sister in Europe." I motioned to Karina, who was standing back, looking *very* irritated. "We came here about a week ago to spend the summer in the city."

"Which ship brought you here?" he asked.

"The Titanic," I said, and, as expected, he leaned forward in further interest.

"I'm thankful that you and your sister arrived unharmed," he said. "And that the wind blew you my way today."

We stood like that for a few seconds, eyes locked, neither of us saying a word.

The last time I'd felt an intense energy like this between a guy had been with Ethan when we'd first met. But unlike those memories with Ethan, what was happening here with William was *real*.

"I'm sorry," he said, shaking his head to refocus. "I didn't introduce myself. I'm William Bradshaw."

"Mira Brown," I said, and he smiled at the sound of my name.

"Mira," he repeated, as if I were a mystery he was determined to solve. "What are your dinner plans tomorrow evening?"

Before I could answer, Karina stalked angrily to my side and linked her arm with mine. "My sister and I are having dinner together tomorrow," she said, an edge of warning in her tone.

"Of course." He nodded. "I wouldn't expect to dine with her without a chaperone."

"Chaperone?" I looked back and forth between William and Karina, confused.

William raised an eyebrow. "Do chaperones not accompany you in Australia while you go out with your suitors?" he asked.

Suitors… another word that caught me by surprise.

William sees himself as my suitor?

"They do," Karina jumped in, and then she turned to me and gave me a small smile. "Mira here simply enjoys toying with people by making Australia sound like an alien planet."

"An alien planet that I can't wait to visit someday," William said mischievously, and then he turned back to me. "I'll pick you up at five?"

"Yes." My cheeks heated—was I actually *blushing* around a guy? "That sounds perfect."

"Where can I find you?"

"We can meet you here," Karina said quickly, at the same time as I said, "The St. Regis Hotel."

I glared at her, annoyed that she wanted us to hide where we were staying, then turned my focus back to William. "We'll meet you in the lobby of the St. Regis."

"I'm looking forward to it."

The butterflies in my stomach flew up to my throat, and my heart leaped in excitement.

I didn't tear my eyes away from his until Karina dragged me around the corner, and she hurried us away until we were out of William's hearing distance. Then she spun me around, her eyes swirling with anger, and scowled at me. "What. Was. That?" she asked.

"I like him," I said, unable to believe it. "After Ethan, I didn't think I'd ever be interested in another man ever again. But... I like him."

"He lives in 1912," she said.

"I realize that."

"He'll be long dead once we return home."

"I know."

She narrowed her eyes, clearly frustrated with me. "*And* we agreed not to make any unnecessary waves in the past," she said. "He's the most sought-after bachelor in the city. What if you're stopping him from meeting the woman who will eventually become his wife?"

"I just used my dragon magic to sink a ship full of some of the most influential people in history," I said. "One courtship is nothing in comparison."

"And what happens when it's time to leave him?"

"Then I'll leave him." I stood straighter, unwilling to back down on this. Because if I was going to be stuck in 1912 for who knew how long, I might as well make the best of it. "What is it that they say? Better to have loved and lost than to never be loved at all?"

It was something like that. And I'd had enough unrequited love to last me for the rest of my life.

"After Ethan, I need this," I said, and I lowered my voice, pleading now. "Please."

Her eyes softened, as if she understood where I was coming from. "Fine," she said. "But I have to accompany you as a chaperone. Otherwise, people will talk. They'll assume you've let William take your virtue."

"My virtue?" I repeated, laughing. "From going out to dinner?"

"It was a different time back then," she said. "But at least you're Australian, so we can pass off your oddities as being because you're a foreigner."

"It seems like William likes my 'oddities,'" I teased.

"Yes," she agreed. "It seems he does. But we'll worry about your courtship later. Because if you don't want to get kicked out of the St. Regis hotel, then we need to find another human to give us his money."

And with that, we were back to business.

22

MIRA

SUNDAY, JUNE 2, 1912

OVER A MONTH.

I couldn't believe I'd been living in 1912 for so long.

More than that, I couldn't believe how lucky I was to have met William.

We were sitting in the nicest restaurant in New York, right in the middle of Central Park. It was decorated with tons of greenery, and just like the fountain where William and I had met, it was nearly impossible to tell that the restaurant was in the middle of a bustling city.

William and I were dining at a table in the center of the room. I'd quickly learned that when someone of his status went to a restaurant, they sat him where people could see him, to let everyone know they were dining at one of the most popular restaurants in the city.

A few women at some of the other tables glared at

me, which I'd grown accustomed to over the past few weeks. They all wanted William to have chosen them, and they had no idea why he was with a foreigner from the wild land of Australia.

In their eyes, I was lower than dirt.

If only they knew *just* how different my home was from theirs. It amused me simply to think about it.

Karina, of course, sat at a table near the wall, where she could keep an eye on me to chaperone my date with William. She was with a female friend of hers—a vampire she'd befriended in the city. Much like current times, there were rogue vampire clans all throughout America, and Karina was happy to have a friend to hunt with.

I heard the click of the camera, and I realized I'd been gazing out the window at the park beyond. I quickly turned my head to William, glaring playfully. "You know I hate being photographed unaware," I said.

"But it's when you're the most beautiful," he replied. "When you let your guard down and forget there are others watching."

"No one's watching me."

"Wrong," he said. "I am. I *always* am. You shine brighter than anyone I've ever met. Whenever you're around, it's impossible for me to take my eyes off you."

His eyes sparkled when he spoke, as if I'd bewitched

him. It was how he always looked at me. With pure, unfiltered love. Like I was the only person on the planet who mattered to him.

Over these past few weeks, he'd quickly become one of the most important people in my life, too.

We might have continued staring at each other forever if the waiter didn't come over with dessert—a chocolate cake for us to share. I picked up the fork to dig in, but before I could, William stood up and dropped down to his knee in front of me.

My breath caught in my chest.

He couldn't be...

"Mira Brown," he said, gazing up at me with pure love. "From the moment your hat blew into my camera lens, I knew you were special. In these past few weeks, I've come to learn just how unique you are. Your spark for adventure is like none I've ever known, and I can't imagine spending my life with anyone but you." He paused, reached into his jacket pocket, brought out a velvet black box, and opened it. Inside was a ring with a single diamond on it—not a large, flashy diamond, but a modest one, although it sparkled with such light that I knew it had to be the highest quality possible.

This can't be happening...

"I love you, Mira," he said. "And I'd be honored if you'd spend the rest of your life with me. So..." He looked down sheepishly, in a way that was so adorably *William*, then beamed back up at me. "Will you marry me?"

Time stood still.

My heart pounded so quickly that I was sure everyone in the restaurant—who were now all staring at us—could hear it.

I couldn't speak.

I loved William—truly, I did. But *married* at seventeen? It was crazy. Like he'd pointed out, we'd only known each other for a few weeks.

Plus, soon I'd leave him forever, and Karina was going to compel him to move on. Just the idea of it made a lump form in my throat, but she and I had already discussed that it was what had to be done.

William would never understand the truth. Yes, he was open-minded... but the truth was an entirely different level of crazy.

Worry crossed his caring eyes, and he gazed up at me in question.

"Mira?" His voice shook slightly when he said my name. "Maybe I should have waited until we were in private. But after I took that photo of you, and you looked so at peace, I thought..."

"It's okay," I said quickly, even though it was anything but okay. "It's just that I can't stay here forever.

You know that. I'm eventually going home, to my family in Australia."

"I'll be your new family, here in New York," he said, still holding the box out so he could remove the ring and place it on my finger. "You know how much I want to see Australia. We can visit your family whenever you want."

"You don't understand." My voice wavered, and I stood up abruptly, panic filling my lungs. "It's more complicated than you can imagine. I'm sorry. Sorrier than you'll ever know. But I can't marry you."

Defeat crossed his eyes, and I worried he was going to break down in the middle of the restaurant.

But he stood up, closed the box, and placed it back in his pocket.

"You love me," he said with so much intensity that it was clear he believed it with all his heart. "I know you do."

"I do love you," I said. "But I can't marry you."

We stood there like that, staring at each other in the middle of the restaurant, and people started to chatter quietly around us.

This would probably make the headline in the papers tomorrow.

Australian foreigner Mira Brown rejects the most eligible bachelor in New York.

Once more, William was going to be swarmed with women who wanted to steal his heart. And maybe one of them would.

Jealousy coursed through me at the thought, and then Karina appeared by my side.

"My sister cannot marry you," she said to William. "Now, if you'll excuse us, we must leave."

"Let me at least accompany you back to the hotel," he said, his eyes begging me to say yes.

I wanted to.

Maybe I could talk to him in private. Explain the truth. See his reaction…

"We can get back by ourselves," Karina said. "Have a good rest of your night."

He turned back to me. "You love me," he said. "I know you do."

"I do," I said. "But it's so much more complicated than that."

"Love isn't complicated," he said. "It's either there, or it's not. And you're my one, Mira. You have my heart forever. So if you change your mind, you know where to find me."

With that, he spun around, left a wad of cash on the table, and stormed out of the restaurant, leaving me in total devastation as he disappeared into the night.

23

GEMMA

FRIDAY, JUNE 25 (PRESENT DAY)

I STEPPED into the meeting area with the round table, scribbled a quick note on the pad of paper waiting there, and sent it as a fire message to Annika.

The Earth Angel appeared seconds later. Annika usually dressed casually—in jeans and t-shirts—but now she wore the black uniform of Avalon's Army. Even though she couldn't leave the island, she looked fierce and ready to fight.

"Tell me everything," she said.

I took a deep breath, unsure where to start. "Nothing that happened today is permanent," I reminded her, although I was reminding myself just as much. Without the constant reminder, I feared I might break. "I'm going to go back in time. I'm going to fix it."

"What happened?"

My heart shattered again as I replayed the past few hours in my mind. All I could do was see everyone die, over and over and over again.

See *Ethan* die.

Annika's eyes softened, and she reached for my hand to comfort me. "Let's sit down."

We sat, although so much adrenaline coursed through my veins that I couldn't keep myself from fidgeting.

"Now," Annika said, as strong and as focused as ever. "Tell me everything. Spare no details. And then, together, we'll figure out how to make it right."

"I'll do it," Annika said once I was done.

"What?"

"I'll help you figure out where you can get the Golden Scepter. And then, once we have it, I'll use it to slay Lucifer."

"That means you'll have to leave Avalon."

Her eyes turned serious. "It does."

"But you're bound to Avalon by your blood," I said. "If you leave..."

"If I leave, Avalon will return to the state it was in when I arrived," she said. "It'll die. Forever. But if I don't do this, we'll have no way to beat Lucifer. The demons will win. All of us will die." Her voice lowered when she said that last part, and she gazed into the fire blazing in the hearth.

"Thank you," I said simply.

But in my heart, I knew she'd volunteer. As Queens, it was our responsibility to do what we needed to stop the demons from taking over our world, no matter how hard those decisions might be. We wouldn't have been chosen by the Holy Objects if we weren't strong enough to make those choices.

"We needed the protection of Avalon as a safe place from the demons," she said. "With Lucifer slain, the island's purpose will be served. *My* purpose as the Earth Angel will be served."

I said nothing, instead staring into the fire with her. Because Avalon was more than a temporary hideout. It was a home to so many people who had nowhere else to go. It was a place where any supernatural could belong, no matter what species they were.

I couldn't imagine—nor could I accept—a world without Avalon.

And that was when it came to me.

A loophole.

In magic, there was *always* a loophole.

"Maybe Avalon doesn't have to die," I said, and hope

flashed in Annika's golden eyes. "I can bring people with me when I travel through time. I can bring *you* with me."

"But when you return to the present, isn't it always a second or so after you left?" she asked.

"It is," I said. "But the first time I time traveled—in the Seventh Kingdom—I only traveled a few minutes back into the past. I didn't have to return to the present because time caught up with itself on its own."

She blinked a few times as she processed what I was saying. "As much as I love fantasy novels, time travel has never been my genre of choice," she finally said. "But you're the Queen of Pentacles. If you say you can do this in a way that a version of myself will always be on Avalon, then let's do it."

"I can do it," I said. "And I will. But first, we need to figure out where we can find the Golden Scepter. And I know what we need to locate it."

"What do you need?" she asked.

"A dragon heart," I said, although when I thought back to the old, used heart we tried to use on the Titanic, I knew what needed to be done. "A *fresh* dragon heart."

"You're going to slay a dragon."

"I won't kill one of my people," I said. "But I will go to them and ask for their help."

"You're going to Ember?"

"Yes."

"How?"

"With magic," I said, and then I walked to the door, put my key in the lock, and stepped into the ivory hall of the Eternal Library.

Hecate wasn't there. I hadn't expected anything else, but it didn't stop disappointment from filling my lungs.

But that was no matter. Because now, I had a mission. I had a *purpose.* And I wasn't going to stop until I got the Golden Scepter and made things right.

So I spun around, put my key back into the lock, and stepped into the meeting hall of the underwater kingdom in Ember.

24

GEMMA

FRIDAY, JUNE 25 (PRESENT DAY)

THE MEETING ROOM was empty when I arrived. I took a deep breath and stared out at the sprawling city below, all of it enclosed in a bubble of air kept in place by the dragons with elemental water magic and air magic.

It was beautiful. The existence of the hidden kingdom of Ember was one of the many wonders of the magical world—a way for the dragons to keep themselves safe from the dark fae and mages that had overtaken their realm.

Most of the candles in the shops and apartments were out, which was the only way to tell what time of day it was, given that sunlight didn't reach the depths of the ocean.

I enjoyed the tiny moment of peace, not knowing when I might have time like this to myself again. A moment when there was possibility in the future—when I could change the fates of the battle that had gone horribly wrong.

Because if I failed…

No, I thought. *I can't fail. I won't fail.*

Decision made, I straightened my shoulders, marched into the hall, and walked to the door that led into the quarters of Hypatia, one of the head elders.

A guard waited at the door—a male dragon with deep blue eyes and dark hair who looked to be in his forties. He'd been in the meeting room when Ethan, Torrence, Reed, and I had first been in Ember—when we'd come to find the first half of the Holy Crown.

He lowered his eyes at the sight of me. "Your Highness," he said. "Welcome back to Ember."

"I need to speak to Hypatia," I said. "Now."

"I'll go wake her."

No questions, and no hesitation. Because as the Queen of Pentacles and the twin flame of their king, I was the highest authority in the kingdom.

My heart hurt again at the thought of their king.

Of Ethan.

They had no idea what had happened to him.

Once I fixed this, they never would.

I waited outside the door, not wanting to take advantage of my authority by bursting into Hypatia's quarters.

She was an elder of the dragon kingdom, and she deserved my respect.

We likely wouldn't have the second half of the Holy Crown right now if not for her help.

A lump formed in my throat at the memory of how she'd slit the neck of the dragon who'd volunteered to sacrifice himself so we could track down the second half of the Crown. Hypatia was strong and brave—a true leader.

I doubted I was strong enough to do what she'd done.

She came to the door in less than a minute. She wore a silk pink robe, and her gray hair was up in a twist at the back of her head.

Since I'd been crowned Queen of Pentacles, Ethan and I had come to Ember multiple times, so Hypatia didn't have to be briefed on what the Crown could do.

Her eyes crinkled in concern when she saw me, and she opened the door wider. "Come in," she said, and I entered her quarters. Another woman was in there—some sort of lady's maid, and Hypatia focused on her. "Bring us some tea," she ordered. Then she looked to me and asked, "What kind do you prefer?"

"Hot chocolate," I said instantly. "The white kind, if you have it."

"I'm sure Priya can find it somewhere."

"On it," Priya said, and then she left the room, leaving me, Hypatia, and the male guard alone.

Hypatia and I sat down on the sofa. The man remained standing.

I looked to him, unsure if he could be trusted.

"Tarren remains by my side at all times," Hypatia said. "You can speak freely around him."

I'd wanted to speak to Hypatia alone, but I didn't have the energy to fight her on this. If she said her guard could be trusted, then I believed her.

"We lost the war," I said, although as I told her, it didn't feel real. Probably because I knew this timeline wasn't going to remain real. "Lilith used the gifted vampire blood to raise Lucifer from his Hell prison. None of us could kill him. Not Raven, or Sage, or Selena… or Ethan."

When I said his name, it came out as a whisper.

Immediately afterward, there was a knock on the door.

Priya had returned with our drinks. She placed steaming hot jasmine tea in front of Hypatia, and a white hot chocolate in front of me.

"I'll leave you alone," she said, clearly understanding that the conversation Hypatia and I were about to have was private.

"Thank you," Hypatia said, and we were both silent until the door clicked behind Priya.

I picked up my hot chocolate—she'd made it perfectly. But even my comfort drink wasn't enough to calm the anxiety and grief racing through my veins, so I placed it back down, ready to continue my conversation with Hypatia.

"King Pendragon is dead," Hypatia said solemnly.

"It's not permanent," I said. "I'm going to change it."

"How?"

I took another sip of hot chocolate, then told her about the Golden Scepter and the plan I'd created with Annika—how Annika had agreed to leave Avalon to kill Lucifer.

Suddenly, Tarren stepped forward.

"I'll do it," he said.

"You'll do what?" I asked.

"You need to locate the Golden Scepter. You have no leads about where it could be, and given the destruction that Lucifer and the demons are likely causing on Earth right now, your resources are limited. The best way to find the Golden Scepter is to use a dragon heart. That's why you're here, isn't it? To request one?"

"It is," I said, since there was no point in lying about it.

Still, the thought of what I was asking of them made my stomach roll over.

It's for the greater good, I reminded myself. *Hundreds—maybe thousands—have already died since Lucifer rose. Sacrifices are necessary in times of war.*

But more importantly, it was going to be okay. Because once I fixed this, none of this would have ever happened.

If I was able to fix this.

No, I instantly thought. It wasn't "if." I *was* going to fix this. There was no way that Fate intended the future to end up this way. I'd been chosen as the Queen of Pentacles for a reason.

I sat straighter as confidence raced through me.

I could do this.

Hypatia eyed Tarren suspiciously. "Are you offering to find a dragon who's willing to sacrifice themselves to find the Golden Scepter?" she asked.

"No," he said. "I'm offering to sacrifice myself so the Queen of Pentacles can use my heart to find the Golden Scepter."

She froze, then pursed her lips in dissatisfaction. "You're my head guard," she said. "I need you here. With me."

I looked back and forth between them, and I realized —she was in love with him. And, even though she was likely two or three decades older than he was, I could tell from the way he was looking at her that he fully returned her love.

"Our king is dead," he said. "There's no reason for anyone to know he's fallen. Gemma can use my heart to find the Scepter so the Earth Angel can kill Lucifer. Once she does, this reality will be erased. King Pendragon will still be alive. *I'll* still be alive."

Hypatia still said nothing.

"I have faith in the Queen of Pentacles," he continued. "I know you do, too."

"As do many others in our kingdom," she snapped. "But this is a job for a soldier. A pawn."

"I am a soldier. I serve the Queen of Pentacles," he said, strong and determined. "I want her to use my heart to locate the Golden Scepter. Locating the Scepter is a pivotal part in winning this war—and it's *my* part. I know it deep in my bones." He turned to me, and I could tell by the look on his face that his mind was made up. "The stronger the magic of a dragon, the stronger the magic of their heart," he said. "I was chosen to guard Hypatia because I'm the best there is. Use my heart. Find the Scepter. Let the Earth Angel kill Lucifer to create a new reality—a reality where we take down the demons for good."

I held his gaze, unable to look at Hypatia. Because

Tarren was right. We needed a strong heart to locate the Golden Scepter.

His offer was the best I could hope for. It was what I'd come here for.

But this decision wasn't up to me.

"I won't be the one to do it," Hypatia broke the silence.

Tarren looked to her, and his eyes turned gentle. "I'd never ask you to."

It was silent again, and I held my breath, not wanting to interrupt this moment between them.

Hypatia nodded in what looked like acceptance, then refocused on me. "Can you leave us for a few minutes?" she asked.

"Of course." I stepped out into the empty hall, leaving them alone.

Ten minutes later, Hypatia opened the door and beckoned me inside. Her eyes were glassy—she'd clearly been crying.

My heart ached for her nearly as much as it did for my grief over Ethan.

Hypatia moved closer to Tarren and took his hand. "The next time you see us, we won't remember this timeline," she said to me.

"Correct."

"So when it's all over, and you've fixed the past, I

want you to tell me what happened," she said. "I want you to come to me and Tarren and tell us about the sacrifice he made in this timeline to help save the world."

I looked to Tarren to make sure it was okay.

"I don't expect glory or validation," he said. "But Hypatia insists, and therefore, I ask this of you as well."

"You have my word," I promised.

"Thank you," he said. "Now, there's one final thing we request."

"Tell me, and I'll do my best to honor it," I said, since I'd learned to never promise something before knowing what a person was asking of me.

"I want you to be the one to wield the blade and end my life."

25

GEMMA

FRIDAY, JUNE 25 (PRESENT DAY)

My blood felt like it froze in my veins, and for a moment, I couldn't breathe.

"You want me to kill you." I prayed I was wrong, even though his request was clear.

"I don't want Hypatia to do it," he said. "And we don't want to involve anyone else in what's going on here. Plus, you're the Queen of Pentacles. It's your job to do what needs to be done to change the present. I'm doing what I need to do by offering myself as a sacrifice. I—" he started, and then he stopped, glancing at Hypatia before looking back to me. "*We* want you to do this for us."

I swallowed, unsure what to say.

Because he was asking me to slit his throat. To watch

his life blood drain out of him, and then cut his heart out of his chest after it stopped beating.

My stomach rolled at the thought.

"May I please have a moment?" I asked Hypatia.

"Of course," she said, and then I hurried to her bathroom, making it just before my stomach revolted against me and emptied all of its contents into the toilet.

Once there was nothing left inside me, I swished my mouth out with water from the sink and gazed at my reflection in the mirror. My eyes were bloodshot, there were circles beneath them, and my skin was pale and dry. Exhaustion felt like a living thing, clawing at my insides and trying to pull me down into its endless spiral of despair.

But the Crown on my head glowed with magic, and that magic flowed through me, warming me with energy that I desperately needed.

The magic of the Crown reminded me who I was.

The Queen of Pentacles.

Being a Queen wasn't all confidence and glory. It meant making hard decisions and doing things I'd never dreamed I could do.

The past day had pushed me to my limits. Now, it was pushing me even more.

But the sad, haggard girl in the mirror wasn't who I

wanted to be. This timeline wasn't one I wanted to exist in.

I had the power to change it. Plus, once everything was fixed, Tarren would still be alive. I never would have killed him.

But I'd still have the memories of what I'd done. This timeline would disappear for everyone else, but it would still exist for me.

It would still exist for Ethan as well. Thanks to our twin flame bond, he also remembered the timelines I'd changed. We'd learned it from Hecate in one of the few times she'd appeared to us in the Library.

Would he remember dying?

The answer came to me immediately—yes. He remembered everything, so he'd remember dying as well.

He'd also know that I saved him. He was going to ask how I did it. And I was going to tell him everything.

What I was about to do to Tarren wouldn't be a burden I'd have to bear alone. Ethan would help me learn how to live with it.

I *had* to do this. Not just for Ethan, but for everyone.

I was the Queen of Pentacles, and I refused to let the world down. More than that—I refused to let *myself* down.

And so, I cupped my hands together and drank some water from the sink, relieved when it settled in my stomach without coming back up. Then I straightened and stared at myself in the mirror again. There was a strength and determination in my eyes that hadn't been there before.

I can do this.

With that final thought, I walked back into Hypatia's living room with my head held high. I pulled my dagger from my weapons belt—the holy weapon I carried with me in case I was confronted with a demon.

"The Queen of Swords taught me how to do this as quickly and painlessly as possible," I assured Tarren, since while Raven was dangerous with a sword, she wasn't cruel. Then I turned to Hypatia, swallowing before continuing. "But I'm going to need you to walk me through what to do afterward."

Meaning: I needed her to tell me how to cut the heart from his chest without damaging it.

"I will," she promised.

"Thank you," I said, and when I met Tarren's eyes, he stared back at me with deep appreciation and kneeled in front of me.

"I'm the one who should be thanking you," he said, and then he nodded at me, like he was saying it was all going to be okay.

Because it *was* all going to be okay.

And so, keeping my eyes locked with his, I took a deep breath, tightened my grip on the handle of my dagger, and did what needed to be done.

26

GEMMA

FRIDAY, JUNE 25 (PRESENT DAY)

Once the heart was removed and placed in a satchel, Hypatia and I kneeled before Tarren's body—which we'd covered with a sheet—held our hands together, and spent a few minutes in prayer.

"Your sacrifice will never be forgotten," she finished, and I gave her a small nod of assurance of my promise that in the new timeline, I'd tell them what had happened in this one.

Then I looked up, imagining the ceiling of the ivory hall of the Eternal Library, and thanked Hecate for gifting me with my magic.

Hypatia squeezed my hands, her eyes full of respect when she looked at me. "You're a true Queen," she said, and then she stood up, picked up the satchel with

Tarren's heart, and handed it to me. "I doubt the Golden Scepter is in Ember, but there's always a chance. So before you leave, try to see if you can sense it."

I reached into the satchel and held Tarren's heart gently in my hand. I'd cleaned it of blood, and I could feel the magic pulsing out of it from my touch.

In the past, Ethan had been the one to use the heart to try to locate the objects we were searching for. He'd tried to spare me from such a gruesome task.

Now, the strong magic that flowed out of Tarren's heart filled me with further confidence that I could do this.

I didn't know exactly how to "use" the heart, so as always, I tuned into my magical instinct and let it guide me.

Where is the Golden Scepter? I thought as I held onto the heart.

Nothing changed.

I tried again, and again, nothing.

"It's not in Ember," I said, releasing the heart.

"As I suspected," Hypatia said. "But I trust that wherever it is, you'll find it."

"I will," I said. "And the next time I see you, it'll be with good news. I promise."

"I'll see you in another life," she said.

"Another *timeline*," I corrected her, and then I walked over to the door that led out of her room, put my key into the keyhole, and stepped back into the Eternal Library.

If Hecate was there, I already knew what I was going to ask: which realm the Golden Scepter was in. But she wasn't there.

I knew she wouldn't be.

So I used my key to go to a place I prayed was still safe from the demons—the tearoom in the Haven.

It was empty, but still intact. Immediately, I reached into the satchel and asked the heart to locate the Golden Scepter.

Just like in Ember, nothing happened.

Please be in the Otherworld, I thought, as if thinking it could make it true. Because the Otherworld was the only other realm I'd ever been to. Since I could only use my key to go to places I'd already been, it was going to be a lot more complicated if the Golden Scepter was in another realm.

But I'd worry about that when the time came. So I used my key to return to the Eternal Library, and then walked into the courtyard of Sorcha's palace.

In the current timeline, where Selena was alive, the Otherworld hadn't fallen prey to the zombies like it had when she'd died. It was bursting with life again, and there wasn't even a barrier dome around it, since the dome's protection wasn't necessary anymore.

The Empress was waiting for me next to the fountain, alongside her main advisor, Aeliana.

The fountain was drained of water. Which meant if someone were to try to enter through the portal, they wouldn't be able to get through. And when I looked around the courtyard, there was another huge noticeable difference—the fae standing along the walls of the palace all had wings. They were dressed in simple robes similar to the ones previously worn by the half-blood slaves, which made it obvious that they worked in the palace, but none of them had the red circle tattoos around their biceps that bound them to servitude.

Because in the past few months, Selena had done as she'd promised—she'd freed the half-blood slaves. There was still a lot of work to be done in restructuring the Otherworld's economy, but the half-bloods were now being paid fair wages for their work.

But discussing the politics of the Otherworld was far from the reason I was here.

"We know what happened with Lucifer," Sorcha said, not even bothering with a formal greeting. "Aeliana tells me you're working to fix it."

"I am," I said, and then I quickly filled her in on what I'd learned about the Golden Scepter.

"I've never heard of a Golden Scepter," she said. "But I hope for all our sakes that you're able to find it."

"Me, too." I reached into the satchel, wrapped my hand around the heart, and asked it to locate the Golden Scepter.

Nothing happened.

My heart dropped, and when I looked back at Sorcha and Aeliana, I could tell they both already knew what had happened.

"You knew this was going to happen before I even tried," I said to Aeliana, since she was a half-blood gifted with the ability of future sight.

"I did," she said.

"So tell me," I said desperately. "What do I need to do next?"

"I don't see all possible futures," she said. "I only see the future your current decision will lead to."

"And what decision is that?"

"Why don't you tell me?" she asked patiently.

I bit my lower lip and thought for a few seconds. "I guess my next move would be to go to Avalon," I said. "Let the Earth Angel know what's going on and see if she can help get me into other realms, so I can try to find the Scepter in those."

"That sounds like a solid plan." She gave me an encouraging smile.

Hope filled me once again, and more importantly, trust in myself.

"Thank you," I told them. "And I promise you—next time I see you, it'll be with good news."

"I know it will be," Aeliana said. "Goodbye, and good luck."

27

GEMMA

FRIDAY, JUNE 25 (PRESENT DAY)

ANNIKA WAS PACING in her quarters when I arrived back in Avalon.

Had she been alone this entire time?

Possibly. One thing I'd learned about the Earth Angel during my time in Avalon was that when Annika was troubled, she tended to isolate herself.

She stopped pacing when she saw me. "We've been waiting for you," she said, and then she hurried into her bedroom and told whoever was in there to wake up.

She came back inside with one of the last people I'd expected to see.

"Torrence." I gasped in surprise, and then I ran forward and hugged her. "I thought you were dead."

She pulled out of the hug and gave me a forced half-smile. "I probably would be dead if I'd stayed there."

"You left Vegas," I said, and she nodded. "When?"

"After Ethan fell, Lavinia used the Dark Wand and killed Reed," she said hollowly. "I knew then that our best chance of winning the battle was for you to go back in time and change everything before it happened. Because this timeline can't be the final one. It just can't."

"It won't be," I assured her, and she nodded, like she already knew it. "But if you left soon after I did, why didn't I see you when I got back to Avalon?"

"I went to my mom's first," she said. "I brought her to the kingdom where I thought she'd be the safest—the Ward. Of course, Makena wanted to know everything that had happened with Lucifer. Once I'd finished filling her in and returned to Avalon, you were already gone."

I nodded, since it made sense. If my mom had been in California instead of in the Haven, I would have immediately gotten her out of there and brought her to one of the kingdoms, too.

Although, I supposed none of it technically mattered, since once we were done here, this timeline would cease to exist.

"I did one more thing before leaving Vegas," she said, and I looked to her to continue. "I grabbed the Dark Sword and took it with me."

"How?" I asked, since the last thing I remembered of the Dark Sword was it soaring into Ethan's heart.

"I ran for it and grabbed it." She shrugged, like it was simple. "It was chaos. Then I flashed out before anyone could catch me."

"And where's the Dark Sword now?"

"Here, on Avalon."

"I'm keeping it somewhere safe," Annika added.

"Good," I said. "As long as the Dark Sword doesn't claim another Queen, we have time to fix this."

"Selena stored the Holy Wand in the ether in her final moments," Torrence said. "So we have nothing to worry about there. The only wild card is Excalibur."

"The Holy Objects are on our side." As I said it, the Crown on my head hummed with magic, as if it was supporting my thought. "It won't claim another Queen without giving us a chance to fix this."

"I hope so," Annika said.

"I know so." I must have sounded confident enough, because she nodded and didn't continue the conversation further.

I turned to Torrence. "There's a weapon that can slay Lucifer," I started, but Torrence interrupted before I could continue.

"Annika told me everything," she said. "Did you get the dragon heart?"

"I did," I said, and I filled them in on what had happened while I was in Ember.

They were silent for a few seconds.

"What you did was tough," Annika finally said. "But it was the right thing to do."

"Except the heart hasn't gotten me anywhere so far," I said. "The Scepter wasn't in Ember, it wasn't on Earth, and it wasn't in the Otherworld. Are there any other realms we can get to? Maybe the mages can bring us to Mystica?"

"Maybe," she said. "But I've been thinking. And I've figured out another way to locate the Scepter."

"What way is that?"

"The same way you located the Dark Sword."

I took a moment to process what she was suggesting.

"Are you saying you've traced the Golden Scepter back in history?" I asked.

"There are no written records of the Golden Scepter," Torrence said. "At least, none that I know of. But just because there are no written records doesn't mean there aren't other ways of tracing it."

"What do you mean?"

"She means that some of the oldest supernaturals live right here in Avalon," Annika said. "The fae who left the Otherworld to live here weren't able to fight against Lucifer because their iron allergy makes it so they can't get to Earth. And before the witches cast the spell on them that made the fae allergic to iron, many of them lived on Earth."

I thought back to what I'd learned in my history lessons back in Utopia. "That was over a thousand years ago," I said.

"These holy weapons are older than that," Annika replied. "As are some of the fae who live here. I don't think it could hurt to ask if any of them came across the Golden Scepter at any point in time."

"Any point in time during or before the Middle Ages." I could barely comprehend such a thing. Because I'd thought 1912 was far back to travel.

That would be nothing in comparison to this.

"How is it any different from trying to go to another realm?" Torrence asked. "Because from what I've heard, Mystica is pretty similar to the Middle Ages—except it would be much harder to navigate, since you're not a mage."

"Good point," I said.

"If this works, I think it's a better option than Mystica," Annika said. "And I've already gathered some of the oldest fae to meet with us. They're waiting at the round table."

"I thought the round table was reserved for the leaders of Avalon," I said.

"The leaders of Avalon are dead. Besides, I make the rules here," she said. "So, let's go find out what they know."

28

GEMMA

FRIDAY, JUNE 25 (PRESENT DAY)

ABOUT THIRTY FAE waited in the meeting room—far too many for them to all sit at the table. So they were standing, chatting amongst themselves and trying to figure out what could have happened in the battle to slay Lucifer.

They silenced the moment Annika, Torrence, and I walked through the door.

Annika walked to the front of the room to face them. Torrence and I stood by her sides. The chairs around the table remained empty—a reminder of those lost in the battle.

My heart ached from looking at the empty chairs.

This timeline will be erased, I reminded myself, and then I focused on the fae standing before us—the oldest fae in Avalon. From their youthful faces—they all appeared to be in their mid to upper twenties—it was impossible to know exactly *how* old they were.

A woman with gold wings and dark curly hair stepped forward, her gaze focused on mine. "The battle didn't go as planned," she said simply. "You need information from us—ancient information—to go back in time and change the outcome of what happened."

"How did you know?" I asked, since Annika hadn't filled them in on what had happened yet.

"Once you get to be as old as I am, it's not too hard to figure these things out," she said. "None of the other rulers of Avalon are here, which I presume means they were either captured or killed. You've gathered the oldest fae in Avalon to meet with you. You have the ability to travel back in time. Which means there's information you think we'll have that will help you change the outcome of the battle against Lucifer and the demons."

"Correct," Annika said, and she launched into telling them the details. "Do any of you know where and when Gemma might be able to locate the Golden Scepter?"

Most of them shook their heads no.

But the golden winged fae curved her lips into a small smile, like she knew something.

I held her gaze, waiting for her to share.

"I heard mention of the Golden Scepter in a city in

Italy where I used to live," she said. "There was a circle of dark witches rumored to have it. But before word could spread, they left and were never heard from again."

"What city?" I asked.

"Pompeii," she said, as if I should have heard of it.

I hadn't. The only cities I knew of in Italy were Rome, Venice, Florence, and Milan.

"What year?" I braced myself for something startling.

"79 AD."

Double digits.

I hadn't braced myself for *that*.

"Ancient Italy," I said, and a slight bit of relief coursed through me, since Ancient Italy was far more civilized than the Middle Ages.

Minus the gladiator fights to the death, of course.

"Does anyone else have any other information?" Annika asked, looking around the room.

No one spoke up.

So, Ancient Italy it was.

29

GEMMA

MONDAY, JUNE 28 (PRESENT DAY)

THE GOLDEN WINGED FAE—LIVIA—SPENT two days briefing us on what to expect in 79 AD.

Now, I was in the meeting room with Torrence, Annika, Livia, and Ruby—a witch who'd been to Pompeii and could teleport us there. Torrence and I wore colorful robes that were popular with nobles of the time. Mine was red, and Torrence's was green. Mine had been fashioned with a large enough pocket to stash the dragon heart, and since the robe was loose, the heart fit inside without being bulky.

Livia reached for the bracelet on her wrist, unclasped it, and held it out to me.

"You really think your past self will believe us?" I asked.

"This bracelet is one of a kind," she said. "It was

forged by my soulmate, Atticus." Her voice wavered when she said his name, since he'd died last year in the plague that had overtaken the Otherworld. "He'll be able to identify his own craftsmanship."

"We wouldn't be able to do this without your help," I said as she clasped the bracelet onto my wrist. It was pure gold, so it was heavier than anticipated.

"I'm simply doing my part to make sure the demons don't take over the realms," she said. "The Otherworld included."

I nodded, since it was a sentiment I'd been hearing a lot recently.

Everyone was counting on me—not just to save Earth, but to make sure the demons didn't invade the other realms, too.

And I wasn't going to let them down.

Torrence reached into the pocket of her dress and pulled out two vials of milky blue liquid. "This will last for twenty-four hours," she said, examining the potion with pride. "Are you ready to try it?"

"Ready as ever," I said, since I just wanted to get to Pompeii, find the Scepter, and get back to Avalon.

Torrence handed a vial to me, looked at me with determination, and we clinked our vials together.

"To understanding dead languages," I said.

"Carpe diem." She smirked, raised the vial to her lips, and downed it.

I did the same.

The blue liquid tasted sweet and thick. As I swallowed it down, my head buzzed, and my mouth did, too. My tongue felt heavy for a few seconds, my ears rang, and then, everything went back to normal.

"Well?" Livia asked with a raised eyebrow. "Did it work?"

"I don't know," I said. "Say something in Latin."

"I just did."

"You mean you asked if it worked in Latin?"

"And you replied in it. This entire exchange has been in Latin."

"Like I promised," Torrence said. "The potion makes it so you understand any language someone speaks to you, and that they hear your response in that language, too."

"Impressive," I said.

"Of course it is." Torrence smirked again. "I made it."

Annika looked around at the three of us. "I assume it worked?" she asked.

"Yes," I said, to test it further. "It worked."

"Good."

"Did I say that in English?"

"You did," Livia replied, since she understood both

languages. "Now, I wish I could accompany you to Pompeii so I could bring you to the exact place where my villa once stood. But the map I made is a good one, so I'm sure you'll find your way."

"I have a good sense of direction," I said, since being in tune with the world around me was one of the benefits of my elemental magic.

"That makes one of us," Torrence said, and this time, I was the one who smirked a bit.

If I was going to go back to the ancient times with someone who wasn't Ethan, I was glad it was Torrence.

"I'm glad you're coming with me," I said, since one big thing I'd learned through all of this was that life was too short to hold back on voicing appreciation for the people you cared about.

"You better be." She winked. "Because who better than a dark half-mage to help you steal an ancient weapon from a circle of dark witches?"

I almost said Ethan, but I held back. Because Torrence's magic was insanely strong—even stronger than that of a full mage. The only person I'd ever seen with magic stronger than hers was Selena.

Ethan, Mira, and I probably would have been killed by the dark mages guarding the entrance to Ember if Torrence hadn't dropped in and saved us.

"There's no one better," I said, meaning it.

The witch—Ruby—stepped forward. Much like the gem she was named for, her hair was a stunning shade of dark red. "Who's coming first?" she asked.

Torrence stepped forward. "I am," she said.

"No," I said. "I am."

"I see you're already on the same wavelength," Ruby said wryly.

"We don't know what's waiting for us in Pompeii," Torrence said. "And I'm expendable. Gemma's not."

I opened my mouth to refute her, but stopped myself. Because given that this timeline was going to be erased, she was right.

Everyone was expendable but me and Annika, since we only needed the two of us—and the Golden Scepter—to slay Lucifer.

"All right," I agreed, and Torrence looked at me with respect. "You go first."

"My pleasure, *Your Highness*," she said with a small curtsy, in a tone that was both joking and full of respect.

Only Torrence would be able to manage that.

"Now," she said, turning to Ruby. "Let's go to Italy."

Ruby took Torrence's hands, and the two of them flashed out.

I held my breath as I waited for her to return.

What if the demons somehow knew we were going there?

What if they're waiting to launch an attack and kill them? What if Lucifer *is there?*

I swallowed down fear at the thought.

Luckily, Ruby returned before I could think about it further.

"Well?" I asked.

"Well, what?"

"Did everything go smoothly?"

"Would I be here otherwise?"

"No," I said, breathing out slowly. Because of course everything was fine. Lucifer and the dark witches had no way to track us. We were too careful for that. And they had no way of guessing we'd go to Pompeii. They had far bigger targets than that. A random city in Italy wasn't a target at all.

But the vampire kingdoms are.

I pushed the thought out of my mind, since my mom was at one of them. If the citizens of the kingdoms needed to go somewhere else to hide, they would. I had to trust that my mom was in good hands with Mary.

And that she was in good hands with me, given that I was the one fixing this mess.

"Gemma?" Ruby asked, holding out her hands. "We should get going. Torrence is going to be irritated if you leave her waiting."

From the way she said it, you'd think Torrence was the Queen instead of me.

"Okay." I reached forward, taking her hands in mine. "Let's go."

One moment we were in the meeting room, and the next, we were in a quaint Italian city.

A burst of power rushed through me when my feet hit the ground. Because there was magic here. Serious, major, *intense* earth and fire magic.

I spun around and saw where the magic was coming from.

A massive volcano loomed over the city. It overtook the skyline, and the bustling buildings of Pompeii were tiny in comparison. And, most noticeably, the volcano wasn't dormant. I could feel the strength of the magma that flowed in the chambers below, like its fire had an invisible tie to my magic. It was like the magma pulsed with the beat of my heart.

"Mount Vesuvius," Ruby said. "One of the most dangerous volcanoes in the world. Anyone careless enough to have lived on its slopes has paid the price."

"But no large eruptions?" I asked.

"Of course not." Ruby chuckled. "Vesuvius's eruptions are short and small. There wouldn't be cities around it otherwise."

"There're enough magma in there to bury all these

cities in ash," I said as I continued to stare at the volcanic monster.

Torrence stepped in front of me, blocking my view of the volcano. "Are you gonna keep staring at that volcano, or are you gonna take us back in time to get the Scepter?" she asked.

I shook my head to snap out of it. "Sorry," I said, and then I reached into the ether, removed the Holy Crown, and placed it on my head.

Torrence's eyes gleamed with excitement.

"You ready?" I asked, even though I could tell by her expression that she was.

"Once we're done with them, those dark witches won't know what hit them," she said, and then she took my hands, her grip firm around them. "Let's show the ancient Romans what we're made of."

I took a deep breath and focused on the Holy Crown.

Take us back to 79 AD, when Livia learned that the dark witches were in Pompeii with the Golden Scepter, I thought, and then the buzz of magic flowed through me, and Torrence and I flickered out.

30

GEMMA

TUESDAY, AUGUST 24, 79 AD

We reappeared on a cobblestone street in front of the entrance of a marble Roman villa. A few people walked nearby—some of them in high quality clothing like me and Torrence wore, and others in more ragged tunics that made it clear they were servants. They blinked and shook their heads as they looked at us, but then their eyes glazed over, and they continued on their ways. It was like they'd had deja vu—not like they'd just witnessed two people materialize in thin air.

Unless humans had magic shoved in their faces, their minds rewired themselves around it to make logical sense of it.

But they could only miss so much. So I quickly reached for the Crown and put it back in the ether.

Then I returned my focus to the wooden door in front of me, raised my knuckles up to it, and knocked.

The door opened, and a human man in a plain white toga studied us, taking in our robes that made it clear we were of higher status than he was. "Good morning," he said. "How may I help you?"

"We're here to see Livia," I said simply, as if he should have already known that.

"She didn't tell me she'd be receiving guests."

"That's because we're not guests. We're family." I flipped over my hand, reached for my magic, and a small flame grew from my palm.

His eyes widened, and he stepped back, like he was afraid my fire might burn him. "You're like my mistress," he said breathlessly. "Goddesses."

"Yes, we're like Livia. And we've come a long way to speak with her." I didn't break my gaze from his.

"We need her help," Torrence chimed in, and she raised her hand as a small bit of purple magic swirled around her fingers. "And we'll be helping her, too."

He bowed his head, like he was afraid to look at either of us, and opened the door wider. "Come wait in the foyer," he said. "I'll find the mistress and tell her of your arrival. But first, would you mind putting that out?" He glanced at my palm, where the flame still danced.

"Of course." I closed my hand into a fist to snuff out the fire, then he nodded in approval and moved over so Torrence and I could walk inside.

The foyer had a small fountain in the center, and colorful murals on the walls. There were benches inside, but Torrence and I opted to stand.

"I feel like I'm back in the Otherworld," Torrence said.

"It looks like the villas in the Otherworld," I agreed. "But there's so much fire and earth magic here, so it doesn't *feel* like the Otherworld."

"The volcano is that intense?"

"It's like a monster hiding beneath the surface. If the people here knew how much power it had, they would be long evacuated."

"Sounds dangerous."

"It's fueling my magic. Making me stronger than ever."

"Good." Her eyes glinted with approval, then flashed with darkness. "Because when we go up against this Scepter, we're gonna need as much magic as possible."

We only waited for ten minutes before the man in the toga returned. "My mistress has readied the morning meal for four people," he said. "Please, follow me."

He led the way down a hall and into the atrium in the

back of the villa. It was like a smaller version of Empress Sorcha's atrium—open to the sky, with a rectangular pool in the center, and lined with columns. The roof was tiled with red, and the shrubbery was well tended to, although there weren't colorful flowers growing out of them like there were in the Otherworld.

Livia reclined on a lounge chair next to a table covered in fruits, breads, and jams. Her dark curly hair fell around her face just like it did when we'd met, but her golden wings were invisible, since the fae used glamour to conceal their wings while they were on Earth.

A man with light brown hair reclined next to her. Judging by the finery of his robe, I assumed he was her soulmate, Atticus.

Livia waited for the servant to leave before speaking. "Our conversation will be private, thanks to the sound barrier spell my witches have placed around the atrium," she said. "But make no mistake—they are watching us. If you try anything against me, you will regret it."

"We've come here for your help," I said. "We won't hurt either of you."

Atticus eyed us warily. "You're shrouding your scents," he finally said. "What type of supernaturals are you?"

"We're witches," Torrence said, since we'd agreed

before coming here to keep it simple. The dragons wouldn't be coming to Earth for centuries—the other supernaturals didn't even know of their existence yet. "Both of us have been gifted with unique magic by the goddess of witchcraft, Hecate."

It was the best story we could come up with to explain Torrence's mage magic and my elemental magic.

"And your names?" Livia asked.

We quickly introduced ourselves.

"Nice to meet you, Gemma and Torrence," she said. "I'm curious to hear why you've come here. But you know our customs. Join us and have a bite of food first."

We reclined on the other two lounge chairs around the tables—I already knew from my time in the Otherworld that the ancient Romans lounged while they ate instead of sitting straight up—and each took a bite of fruit.

Atticus and Livia kept an eye on our every movement.

"Now," Livia said, and she pushed herself up a bit on her chair. "What is it that you came here to ask?"

"We were told you had information on the location of the Golden Scepter," I said.

She raised an eyebrow. "Who gave you this information?"

"You did."

She pursed her lips and narrowed her eyes. "Come again?"

"This is going to sound crazy, but hear me out," I started, and she waited for me to continue. "Like I said, Torrence and I have been gifted with unique magic from Hecate. My gift is the ability to travel through time."

She stared at me in silence.

"Is this some kind of joke?" Atticus finally asked.

"Not a joke," I said. "Like I told you, Livia is the one who sent us here. Well, the future version of Livia. To prove it, she gave me this to show you."

I removed the bracelet and handed it to him.

He was quiet for a full minute as he studied it. Then he looked to Livia. "Your bracelet," he said. "The one I gave you for your most recent birthday. Give it to me."

She snapped the bracelet off her wrist and handed it to him.

He held them up against each other and studied each detail.

"I know my craftsmanship anywhere," he finally said. "This is the same bracelet I made Livia for her birthday. It should be the only one in existence." He handed both bracelets to Livia so she could see.

She took them and studied them, although for not nearly as long as Atticus had. Then she looked to me. "You're saying that a future version of myself told you to find me and ask about the Golden Scepter, and that she —well, *I*—gave you this bracelet so you could prove you were telling the truth?"

"That's exactly what I'm saying."

"Interesting," she said, and she reclined further back in her chair. "Please, continue. Because this sounds like a fascinating story."

We spent a few hours going through everything with Livia and Atticus. By the time we were finished, it was mid-morning.

Livia was quick to process and believe everything I was telling her.

Atticus was a harder sell, but he eventually came around.

"Where was I through all of this?" he finally asked.

"I mentioned the plague that hit the Otherworld," I said with trepidation. "You fell ill to it."

"It killed me."

"It did. But like I said, I came here to change the future. Now that you know about the plague, you can take precautions to change your fate."

"Simply the information to save Atticus's life would be enough incentive for me to help you," Livia said. "To make things clear, all you're asking for is the location of the dark witches who have the Golden Scepter?"

"Correct."

"All right," she said. "You have done me a great favor by sharing your knowledge of the future. As repayment, I will give you the location of the dark witch circle."

I had a feeling she would have shared their location with us no matter what, but fae were sticklers for not doing anything for free.

"This knowledge will help us greatly," I said, since thanking a fae—even one as kind and gracious as Livia—would bind me to a favor.

"I'm more than happy to share it," she said, and then she told us the location of the dark witch circle.

"As a fair warning, after we leave to find them, I recommend having your witches teleport you, Atticus, and everyone else in your household far away from here," I said.

"Why's that?"

"Because Torrence and I are going to use every magical ability of ours to fight. We'll do *anything* to get that Scepter. And if there's any fallout, I don't want you to be here to suffer the consequences."

31

GEMMA

TUESDAY, AUGUST 24, 79 AD

Livia and Atticus had their human driver take us to the dark witches' villa on their cart, which was pulled by two oxen.

It was a large villa on the outskirts of the city, on the side closer to Vesuvius. Like most of the other villas in Pompeii, it was white with columns, and had a red tiled roof. Nothing about it made it apparent that a circle of dark witches that owned an ancient holy weapon lived there.

Torrence held her hand to her forehead like a visor—it was almost noon, and the sun shined bright overhead. "Are you sure this is the place?" she asked our driver.

"I'm sure."

I reached into my robe, wrapped my hand around the dragon heart, and asked for the location of the

Scepter. The heart pulsed in my grip, and I felt a pull toward the villa.

"This is the right place," I said to Torrence, and I stepped out of the cart to face the driver. "Thank you for taking us here."

"I'll wait for you right here," he said.

"We can get back on our own," I said, since the moment Torrence and I got our hands on that Scepter, I'd bring us back to the present. "You should return to Livia's villa."

"Are you sure?" He looked around warily, like he was worried he'd get in trouble for leaving us alone.

"It's for your own safety."

He furrowed his brow in confusion.

This was one of those moments when I wished I could compel people, like the vampires could.

"Trust me," I tried again. "We'll be fine."

My tone must have been convincing, because he nodded, then steered the oxen to bring the cart back into the city.

Torrence and I turned back toward the villa.

"Time for the barrier spell." She rubbed her hands together excitedly. "Gotta make sure the witches can't blink out of here with that Scepter."

"Is there anything I can do to help?"

"It's no secret that your strength isn't your witch magic," she said with a wink. "I've got this."

Before I could reply, she started chanting the barrier spell in Latin. Except this time, because the language potion was making me *understand* Latin, it sounded like she was speaking the spell in English.

Her purple magic gathered around her, then exploded out of her hands in a dome that surrounded the villa. We were just inside the edge of it.

A butterfly flew inside the dome, but when it tried to fly out, it was stuck. That was how prison domes worked—anything could enter, but once inside, they couldn't leave.

Within seconds, the main door of the villa swung open, and two witches dressed in navy robes stood there, staring us down. They both had light red hair—they looked like mother and daughter—and they looked *pissed*.

"Who are you?" the older one asked.

"My name is Gemma Brown." I raised my hands up and created flames that came up from the tips of my fingers, so they looked like extensions of my nails. "I've come for the Golden Scepter."

"We don't know what that is," the younger one said, although from the way her voice wavered, it was clear she was lying.

Torrence's eyes flashed black. "Wrong answer," she said, and then she held up her hands, her palms facing the witches, and blasted black smoky magic toward them.

They didn't have time to scream before they collapsed to the ground.

I froze in shock. "They didn't try to fight us," I said. "Did you really have to *kill* them?"

Torrence rolled her eyes. "I didn't kill them," she said. "I just knocked them out for a few hours, since they didn't seem interested in helping us. Not that we need their help, since we're close enough to the Scepter that the dragon heart can direct you straight to it."

She was right.

I pulled the fire back inside myself, reached into my robe, and held onto the heart.

"Come on," I said, and I marched inside the villa.

Torrence followed quickly at my heels.

The heart led me into the atrium, where a tall witch with light red hair that matched the other two in the circle stood in the center.

She held a long rod with a sharp, pointed golden crystal at the end.

The Golden Scepter.

"I assume you're here for this?" she said with a knowing smirk.

And that was when I noticed—she wasn't a witch. Her eyes were gold, like Annika's.

She was an angel.

Another Earth Angel.

"You assume correctly," Torrence said, and then she blasted her black smoky magic at the angel.

The Scepter's crystal glowed, and Torrence's magic didn't touch the angel. It was like the Scepter had created a barrier spell around her.

"Mage magic," the angel said. "Interesting."

"You know about mages?" I asked, since we didn't learn much of anything about the mages until recently.

"They want the Scepter," she said simply. "And they've offered me a tempting reward if I give it to them."

That's where the Scepter disappeared to, I realized. *Mystica.*

"What kind of reward?" I asked.

"Living on Earth is torturous for me," she said. "All of the humans with their negative emotions surrounding me all the time. I soak it up like a sponge, until it's all I can feel. Emotions like that consume me on a level you can never understand. So in exchange for the Scepter, the mages have offered me a home in Mystica."

"Why do you think Mystica will be any better for you than Earth?" Torrence asked.

"*Anything* will be better than living on Earth."

"Except I *am* a mage," Torrence said. "And I promise you that our emotions are just as strong as the humans. Maybe stronger. I promise you don't want to live there."

"You're lying."

"I'm not."

The angel held up the Scepter and ran toward Torrence with rage in her eyes. From her expression, it was clear that she was aiming to kill.

Torrence quickly moved to the side, so the angel missed her.

Having missed Torrence, she now set her eyes on me.

So I reached for my fire magic, gathered it, and shot two blasts of it at the angel—one from each of my palms.

The fire didn't go straight like it should have. Instead, it diverted *around* her.

I stared at my hands in shock. As I did, frustration rose within me, and I blasted as much fire at her as I could manage. A roaring ball of it surrounded her— enough fire to char her to the bones.

But when the fire died down, she was still there, unscathed.

She cackled when she saw my shocked expression. "Your magic can't hurt me as long as I hold onto the Scepter," she said.

Anger swirled inside me. We didn't have time for

this. And I wasn't sure how Torrence and I would do if we tried to use our swords and daggers against an angel wielding the Golden Scepter. Probably not well.

Which meant it was time for Plan B.

It wasn't hard to tune into the power of Vesuvius. My fire and earth magic had been aching to do it since teleporting into Pompeii. There was so much fiery magma beneath the surface that the ground pulsed with it. Within seconds, my magic connected to it, like a magnet that had gotten hold and wouldn't let go.

The ground tremored—a small earthquake. It didn't shake me, but the angel's golden eyes flashed with alarm.

"You did that," she realized.

"I did." I nodded as more power rushed through me, and the world shook again, hard enough for cracks to form in the concrete walls around us. "Maybe our magic can't directly hurt you. But that volcano can."

32

GEMMA

TUESDAY, AUGUST 24, 79 AD

"You can't know that," the angel said.

"Vesuvius is one of the most destructive volcanoes in the world," I said. "I felt the intensity of its power the moment I arrived in Pompeii."

"I'm immortal." She raised her chin higher. "A volcano doesn't scare me."

"I know another Earth Angel," I said. "She's immortal, but she can still be killed."

"She doesn't have the Golden Scepter protecting her."

Her confidence was going to cost her life. I could feel it as much as I could feel the earth and fire connected to my soul.

"Have you ever heard of the Golden Scepter going up

against a force of nature like Vesuvius?" I asked, and this time, the world did more than shake.

It exploded with a BOOM so loud that it felt like it shattered my brain. The vibration rose from the ground and rattled every bone in my body. It was like an atomic bomb had gone off.

Within seconds, a black cloud covered the sky, and it was like it had gone from day to night.

Ash.

Flakes of it floated down to the ground like dirty snow, leaving streaks of gray in anything that crossed their path.

True fear crossed over the angel's eyes, and her grip tightened around the Scepter. She looked to Torrence. "Remove the boundary dome," she said. "Your friend might be able to survive the volcano, but you can't."

"I can protect Torrence," I said, since the magma was at my beck and call—I could mold it however I wanted. "But I'm here for the Scepter. If you won't hand it over to me, then I'll pry it away from your ashen corpse."

It was gruesome. But I didn't care. If this was what it took to save Ethan, my family, my friends, and everyone else in the universe, then so be it.

The thought of everyone who would die in the path of the lava made my stomach twist with nausea. But if I didn't do this, there'd be nothing to return home to.

I was sacrificing the lives of an entire city in exchange for saving everyone in the present world. It pained me as much as always, but it needed to be done.

There was another boom, and lightning flashed in the ash cloud overhead.

"Gemma," Torrence said cautiously. "Are you sure you can do this?"

"I *know* I can do this."

"Okay." She moved closer to my side. "I trust you."

I returned my focus to the angel. She was gripping the Scepter so tightly that her knuckles turned white. "I can already feel the lava coming closer," I said. "Hand over the Scepter now, and Torrence will remove the boundary dome. You'll be free to teleport out of here and avoid the disaster to come. And I promise you—it will be a disaster unlike anything you've ever seen."

The ground shook again, like it was confirming my statement. Screams filled the air—cries from all around the city, so shrill that goosebumps covered my skin. Streaks of ash lined both Torrence's and the angel's faces. I was sure mine looked the same.

It was the war paint of the Earth.

Rocks fell from the sky and clattered to the ground. I was able to use my magic to stop them from hitting me and Torrence, but a sharp piece of it sliced the angel's arm. She gasped in pain, and golden blood bubbled up under the cut.

Her eyes glowed gold, and the pointed crystal on the Scepter glowed, too.

I studied her, keeping my gaze locked on hers. "What's your name?" I asked, the question followed by a bright flash of lightning.

"Why do you want to know?"

"Because after you die in this eruption, I want to know the name of the angel I killed."

As I spoke the words, I couldn't believe they were coming out of my mouth. I didn't sound like *me*.

I sounded like a Holy Queen set on vengeance. And while it scared me, it also felt right to embrace the warrior inside me.

My magic felt stronger because of it.

And letting out my rage after witnessing our loss against Lucifer felt like releasing the pain that had been building inside me since seeing Ethan die. It numbed me to it.

"I'm Seraphina," the angel said. "And I'm not going down without a fight."

She ran toward me with the pointed end of the Scepter, but the moment I saw her move, the ground rumbled and shook strongly enough to knock her off her feet.

She smacked to the ground, but kept the Scepter in her hand. It was like it was glued to her palm.

When she looked up at me, her expression was livid.

The Earth was shaking so much that the tiles were breaking from the roof, clacking against each other like shattering glass as they fell to the ground.

Fire exploded from the inside of the house, the flames dancing along the soot-covered roof.

I steadied myself, reached for Torrence's hand, and gripped it tightly as she started to mutter an incantation—the one for the smaller boundary dome around us that could move with us. Only a mage could create a boundary spell strong enough to do that.

The ground continued to tremble, roaring as an avalanche rushed down the volcano.

"You're too late," I told Seraphina, and then lava flowed through the villa, consuming everything in its path.

Everything except for me and Torrence.

It was like we were inside a protective barrier, except it wasn't a barrier—it was Torrence and I using our magic to keep the lava from touching us. I controlled the lava so it didn't hit the barrier walls, since while barrier spells were strong, neither of us knew if they'd been tested against lava before. The boundary also protected us from the heat, which would surely cook

Torrence as if she was inside an oven set at the highest temperature.

The lava started to solidify around us, and I created a flame in my palm so we could see.

The air inside the dome was still. It would have been silent, if not for our ragged breathing and pounding hearts.

"Well?" Torrence finally said. "Did it work?"

"There's only one way to find out." I reached for the dragon heart within my robe and asked it to find the Scepter, since it was impossible to see through the lava. Immediately, I felt a pull forward.

"This way." I called on my earth magic and used it to push the lava aside so we could walk through. It hissed and popped as it moved, parts of it still red with heat.

The boundary dome moved with us, and I pushed through the lava as quickly as possible, since the air inside the boundary dome was limited.

We needed to get the Scepter and get out.

It didn't take long before something poked at the edge of the boundary dome—the pointed end of the Golden Scepter's crystal. It couldn't pierce the dome, and the crystal was no longer glowing. But to bring the Scepter back, I needed to have a firm grip on it. So I connected to my earth magic and pushed a little bit more through the rock, revealing the top part of the rod.

A burned, gnarled hand was wrapped around it.

Seraphina's hand.

"Is she dead?" Torrence asked, and for the first time, she looked scared.

"I don't know. But she's not healing." I pulled the Holy Crown out of the ether, placed it on my head, then reached out of the boundary dome.

It was like sticking my hand into an oven. Heat couldn't hurt me, but this was a level of hot that was beyond uncomfortable. Plus, I was getting dizzy. We were starting to run out of air.

So I gripped the Scepter's rod, right above Seraphina's hand. Then I used my other hand to hold onto Torrence's.

Take us back to the present, I told the Crown.

Magic hummed through me, extending to both Torrence and the Scepter, and we flickered out.

33

GEMMA

MONDAY, JUNE 28 (PRESENT DAY)

CRUMBLED RUINS SURROUNDED US.

Gone were the modern buildings that had been in Pompeii when we'd left.

Instead, parts the villa had been preserved to look like they'd been on the day I'd made Vesuvius erupt.

People walked around in touristy clothes—khakis, t-shirts, and backpacks. A group of girls in their twenties gathered in front of a row of columns to take selfies. The frescos on the outdoor walls were maintained well enough that they were identical to what they'd looked like back in 79 AD, although they'd dulled with time.

Most surprisingly, there were plaques on the walls with writing on them. It was like we were in an outdoor museum.

Vesuvius towered in the distance, but instead of one crater, there were two.

An entirely new crater had formed on the top of the volcano because of the eruption.

As I was staring at it, a heavyset couple who'd been outside long enough to have patches of sweat on their shirts approached us.

"Where's the nearest bathroom?" the man asked.

"I don't know," I said on instinct.

"Oh." He frowned. "I thought you worked here." He glanced up and down my robes, and I realized that not only was I still wearing clothes fit for Ancient Rome, but that I had the Crown on my head and was holding the Golden Scepter.

I breathed out in relief that the Scepter had come through time with us.

Torrence pointed at doors that opened to the atrium. "Just through there and to the left," she said, and the tourists thanked her and headed in that direction.

"They excavated Pompeii," I said, looking around in shock. "And made it into a *museum.*"

"Seems that way." Torrence shrugged. "Is the Scepter intact?"

I studied the golden crystal. It wasn't glowing, but it seemed okay. "I think so," I said.

"That's going to have to be good enough," she said,

and then she grabbed my hands and teleported us back to the meeting room in Avalon.

Everyone was where we'd left them. But not just *everyone*. Livia was there—with Atticus.

He smiled warmly when he saw me. "Livia and I were careful when the plague hit the Otherworld," he said. "I wouldn't be alive right now if it wasn't for you."

I didn't have time to reply before memories of the new timeline flooded my mind.

In this timeline, everyone knew about Pompeii. It was famous for when Vesuvius had erupted in 79 AD, and it was the location of some of the best preserved ruins in the world. As we'd seen when we'd come back to the present, it was an extremely popular tourist destination.

When Livia had told us that she knew the dark witches were in Pompeii, Torrence and I had purposefully chosen the day of the eruption to travel back to. We figured we could trap the witches in their villa and use the eruption to scare them into handing over the Scepter.

Once we fixed the past and slayed Lucifer, I'd tell them the *real* story about how we'd gotten the Scepter.

"It worked," Annika said when she saw us, and she hurried forward, her hand outstretched to take the

Scepter. But she paused when she was inches away. "May I?"

"Of course," I said, and I handed the Scepter to her.

Her hand wrapped around the rod, and the crystal glowed so it was the same color as her golden eyes. "I can do some serious damage with this thing," she said as she studied the Scepter.

"Like slaying the shit out of Lucifer," Torrence said.

"Exactly." Annika nodded and gave Torrence a knowing smile. Then she looked back to me. "You should go change. You can't leave Avalon dressed like that."

I glanced down at my Roman robes, which were covered in soot from the eruption. I couldn't imagine what those tourists must have thought. Probably that I was one of those people who re-enacted ancient times.

"For sure," I said, and I hurried to my room and changed into the black uniform of Avalon's army.

Once dressed, I faced the mirror and studied my reflection. I was a different person than I'd been months ago.

I'd caused enough destruction to turn an entire city into a museum two thousand years later.

I was stronger than I'd ever believed I could be.

But this war was far from over. So I touched the

Holy Crown for good luck and hurried back to the meeting room.

Torrence was still in her soot-covered robes, since her part in our mission was complete. She was talking to Livia and Atticus, already telling them about our adventure in Pompeii and how I'd been the one to make Vesuvius blow its lid.

Annika didn't appear to be listening to Torrence. Instead, she was studying the Scepter, deep in thought. "I guess this is it," she said, and then she focused on me. But she didn't look sad—she looked determined. "Time for me to leave Avalon."

"It's going to be okay," I told her. "We have a plan."

"Plans don't always go as expected," she said. "But I hope for everyone's sake that this one will. Now, are you ready to go?"

"I am," I said, and she took one of my hands—holding onto the Scepter with the other—and teleported us out of Avalon.

We arrived in a small house on the coast of Norway —the one the three mages had lived in nearly twenty years ago, before they'd gone to Avalon to help Annika rule the island. We'd chosen the spot because the magic the mages had used to conceal the house was still active. There was a table and chairs in the main room, but other than that, it was abandoned.

A second after we arrived, Annika screamed and keeled over, her shriek filling the air. She was grabbing her abdomen, and the Scepter had fallen onto the floor.

I ran over to comfort her, but she pushed me away.

Her screams stopped, but her breaths were heavy, and her face was covered in sweat.

I wanted to ask if she was okay. But I didn't, since she clearly wasn't. Instead, I stood there, waiting.

She was strong. She could handle this.

Slowly, she reached for the Scepter, picked it up, and stood straight. The gold in her eyes had dimmed, but it was still there.

"My bond to Avalon has been severed." Her voice was pained as she spoke, and her face was pale. She looked like she could fall over at any second.

"You can't fight like this," I said.

"I can't," she agreed. "We get one shot at this. We have to do it right."

"So we rest?"

"Yes," she said. "We rest."

She led the way to the bedroom, which had three twin beds inside. The blankets were coated with dust, but Annika didn't care. She collapsed into one of them, Scepter still in her hand, and instantly fell asleep.

34

GEMMA

TUESDAY, JUNE 29 (PRESENT DAY)

I WOKE before Annika the next day, and my stomach rumbled. Loudly. But not loudly enough to wake her.

With Lucifer released, it was too dangerous to go to any of the vampire kingdoms for food, and I didn't want to risk going to the café either. So I used my key to go to the next best place—McFly's Tavern. Ethan and I had liked to go to dinner there last fall, before I'd gotten my magic.

Last fall felt like *ages* ago.

I didn't have a credit card on me, so I went inside the kitchen and grabbed two burgers from underneath the heat lamp.

A waiter caught me and widened his eyes. "What are you doing with that?" he asked, but before he could approach, I balanced both plates with one hand, reached for my key, and stepped back into the Library.

Just like a few minutes ago, Hecate wasn't there. So I used my key again and stepped into the kitchen of the Norway house, so I didn't disturb Annika. Luckily, the plumbing still worked, and I poured myself a glass of water and downed it.

I was on my second glass when Annika entered the kitchen.

"You got food," she said, and then she walked over to the table, sat down, and took a huge bite out of one of the burgers.

Disgust crossed her face as she chewed.

"What's wrong?" I asked, and the worst possibilities crossed my mind. Did the demons somehow know I'd be there to grab those burgers? Had they poisoned them?

She chewed slowly, then swallowed, like she was force feeding herself. "It's been nearly two decades since I've had regular food," she said. "I suppose nothing can compare to mana."

I chuckled, even though my mana sometimes tasted like the burgers from McFly's, since I loved them so much. "I guess not," I said, then I took my seat and took a bite of my burger.

I immediately understood the problem.

"Well done," I said, and I scrunched my nose. "Don't judge McFly's on this. Their burgers are *much* better medium rare."

"Don't worry about it," she said. "I know you didn't have time to be picky."

"I took the burgers from under the heat lamp and ran."

"Better than taking half-eaten ones from someone's table," she said with a small smile, and we polished off the rest of the burgers in silence.

Her eyes returned to their regular golden glow.

"How are you feeling?" I asked her.

"Ready to go."

We stood up, and just like when we teleported here, Annika took one of my hands in hers and held the Scepter with the other.

Take us back one week, I told the Crown, and we flickered out, reappearing back in the house that looked exactly the same as it had when we'd arrived yesterday.

35

GEMMA

MONDAY, JULY 21 (EIGHT DAYS AGO)

Annika took a few seconds to adjust, since it was the first time she'd time traveled.

She seemed relatively unfazed.

"Did it hurt?" I asked, since it hurt *everyone* the first time they traveled back in time.

"It was nothing compared to when I severed my bond with Avalon."

Not a yes, but also not a no.

"It only feels like that the first time," I reminded her. "From now on, it'll feel like teleporting."

"Got it," she said, and then she got straight down to business. "Let's go to the Vale first."

I wasn't surprised she'd chosen the Vale, since it was where she'd lived the year before becoming the Earth Angel.

She took my hands and teleported us outside the Vale's boundary dome. The witches on guard widened their eyes when they saw us, and they teleported us inside without any questions.

Once inside the dome, they went down to their knees and lowered their eyes. "Your Highnesses," the older one said, and then she slowly looked up at us. "What can we do for you?"

"We're going to the throne room," Annika said. "Send a fire message to King Alexandra and Queen Deidre to let them know we're here."

"Of course," she said, and then Annika took my hand again and teleported us to the throne room.

King Alexander and Queen Deidre entered a minute later, dressed in the finery expected of the rulers of the Vale. Their eyes widened when they saw Annika.

"It's true," Deidre said, and she hurried closer to Annika, as if making sure she was actually there. "You left Avalon."

"I did," Annika confirmed.

"But the island…"

"I severed my bond with it," Annika said. "But not in the present. In the future."

"A week in the future, to be exact," I added, and then we told them everything that was going on.

After speaking with King Alexander and Queen Deidre, Annika and I went to the Haven, then the Ward, the Carpathian Kingdom, and lastly, the Tower. The ruler of each kingdom listened closely as we filled them in on what was happening, and they promised to help in any way they could.

The kingdoms didn't always get along—especially the Tower—but against Lucifer, we stood together as one.

Once finished, we returned to the house in Norway.

"That went well," Annika said.

"It did," I agreed.

We stood in silence for a few seconds. Because there was still one place to go—but it was a place I needed to go alone.

Once I returned, Annika would be slightly different from the one I was looking at now.

"Are you sure your witch magic is strong enough for you to teleport to Avalon?" Annika asked. "I can always bring you there and avoid running into my past self."

"Don't worry," I said, and I reached for the key around my neck. "I've got this."

Without any further explanation, I walked to the

door that led out of the house, put the key in the lock, and stepped into the ivory hall of the Eternal Library.

Hecate wasn't there.

I was fine with that. Because I was starting to realize that when Hecate wasn't there, it meant she trusted I could handle the situation alone. And she wasn't the only one who trusted this plan. *I* trusted it, too.

I spun back around, put the key into the lock, and walked into an empty bedroom inside Avalon's castle. Before we'd left the island, Annika had brought me there so I'd be able to return. The room was at the end of the hall, and no one had ever lived there.

I removed the folded note from my pocket—the one Annika had already written to tell herself to meet me in the room. She'd said she'd recognize her handwriting anywhere, and I immediately understood why—she had terrible penmanship.

I placed it in my palm and sent it as a fire message to the Annika of this time.

She teleported into the room less than a minute later and studied me suspiciously. "Gemma," she said hesitantly. "I was just training with you on the field."

"You were training with the version of me from your present," I said. "I've come to see you from eight days in the future."

"What happened?"

"In three days, Lilith is going to raise Lucifer," I started, and then I told her all the gory details of what was going to happen in the battle.

"We have to tell the other kingdoms," she said once I was finished. "Let them know to get ready to fight."

"You and I have already alerted them. They're waiting for you to reach out so you can formulate a plan."

"I went to see them with you?" she asked, confused.

"You did."

"But I can't leave Avalon."

"Technically, you can. But if all goes well, this version of you—the you I'm speaking with now—will never leave Avalon. The version of you from the future will kill Lucifer."

From there, I told her about the Golden Scepter and the choice she'd make in a few days.

"I see," she said once I'd finished. "It's a good plan."

"I figured you'd think so, since you helped me make it," I said. "But you're not the only one from this timeline who won't leave Avalon for the battle. I took a risk by observing the battle the last time in case I was the only one left alive who saw it, so I could travel back in time and try to fix it. But your future self and I agreed it wouldn't be logical for me to take that chance again. We don't know what happens to my counterparts if they die, and we can't risk finding out now."

"I understand," she said. "I'll make sure she stays back with me."

"Thank you."

"No," she said. "Thank *you*. Without you, we wouldn't have this chance to make things right."

"I'm just using the gift I was given," I said. "Anyone would do the same in my shoes."

"They'd want to," she said. "But when it came down to it, *could* they?"

A lofty question.

"I don't know," I finally said.

"Well, I do. You were chosen as the Queen of Pentacles for a reason. This is going to work. I can feel it."

"I hope so."

Her golden eyes shined with determination. "I won't accept anything other than success."

"Me either," I agreed, since that was why I was here. "I refuse to believe that Fate wants the demons to win. We can do this."

We stood there for a few seconds in silence, taking in the enormity of what was to come.

"I should get back," Annika eventually said.

I wracked my mind for anything I might have left

out during our conversation, but I was pretty sure I'd covered everything.

"Good luck," she said. "Tell my counterpart that I know she's got this."

"Will do," I said, and then Annika teleported out, and I returned to the house in Norway, where the future version of her—the one from my present—was waiting.

36

GEMMA

THURSDAY, JUNE 24 (FOUR DAYS AGO)

AFTER THREE DAYS OF WAITING, it was time. Again.

The day Lilith was going to raise Lucifer.

During those three days, a huge part of me had wanted to reach out to the people I loved. Ethan. Mira. My mom.

But I didn't. Because I'd see them all after we won the battle. Seeing them now would only cause pain and distraction.

Those were the last things any of us needed.

Instead, Annika and I had hunkered down in the house in Norway. We tried to think of everything that could go wrong with the plan, and how we'd fix it if it did. We had the gift of being prepared, and we weren't going to waste it.

Annika only left once—when she'd disguised herself

and had a witch teleport her to the Vegas Strip to show her where Lilith had raised Lucifer. She'd only needed to stay there for a second to ensure she could return when the moment was right.

The Vegas Strip was so packed with tourists that as far as we were aware, none of the supernaturals keeping watch had noticed her. Even if they'd noticed a rogue supernatural, they'd never guess it was Annika. The last thing they'd expect was for the Earth Angel to have left Avalon. Most people didn't even know it was *possible* for her to leave Avalon.

Finally, it was time to battle Lucifer.

And this time, we were going to win.

37

ANNIKA

THURSDAY, JUNE 24 (FOUR DAYS AGO)

The moment the fire message arrived, I teleported out of the house in Norway, leaving Gemma there. I'd return for her later. First, I had a demon king to slay.

The Strip was a disaster scene. Piles of ash—slain demons—covered the pavement. Gifted vampire blood had rained down on the entire area, and the metallic scent of it stung the back of my throat so strongly that I was overwhelmed by the taste. It was like swallowing pennies.

And that wasn't the only thing I was overwhelmed with.

Because the pain everyone was experiencing during the battle hit me like a million pins being stabbed into my body at once.

It's all in your mind, I thought. *FOCUS. The world is depending on it.*

Raven and Sage finished killing the last of the hellhounds with their Swords. Selena helped as well, using the Holy Wand as a weapon. She moved with incredible grace—an unstoppable force as fierce as the Queens of Swords.

Pride surged through me at the sight of how strong my daughter had become since claiming her place as the Queen of Wands.

Then a giant, terrifying demon with long black claws rose out of the ground.

Lucifer.

Raven and Sage stared him down, their Swords held high. Selena moved behind them. None of them made a move to attack.

Lilith stood behind Lucifer, and even she looked slightly scared.

"Kill them," she said, and Lucifer smirked as he zeroed in on Raven.

In the battle Gemma had told me about, Raven had used this moment to run at Lucifer and try to slay him with Excalibur.

But she knew better this time.

Now, she stayed where she was.

Instead, I ran toward Lucifer, leaped into the air to

fly in an arc toward him, and pulled the Golden Scepter out from the inside of my robes so quickly that he didn't have time to process it as I speared the golden crystal through his heart.

He roared, his eyes glowing bright red, and disintegrated into a pile of ash.

I fell to my knees in front of the pile, holding tightly onto the Golden Scepter.

All the anguish that I'd blocked out when I'd arrived flooded through me again.

This was the reason why angels couldn't live on Earth. Our heightened empathy absorbed all the conflict and pain felt by those who lived here. It was too much. I felt like I was going to explode from the intensity of it.

I couldn't stay here.

Luckily, my part was done.

It was time to get out.

The last thing I saw before teleporting back to the house in Norway were Lilith's angry red eyes as she ran toward me, ready to kill.

38

SAGE

THURSDAY, JUNE 24 (FOUR DAYS AGO)

ANNIKA FLASHED out before Lilith could reach her, and Lilith fell into the pile of Lucifer's ashes.

But while Lilith was powerful, she wasn't the most dangerous force we were up against.

That title went to Lavinia.

Raven was currently facing Lavinia, using Excalibur to deflect the Dark Wand's red magic to keep it from hitting her.

Lavinia's face flushed as she put as much magic as she could muster into the beam of magic.

Raven continued to hold her off.

But Raven couldn't kill Lavinia while she was busy stopping her magic. And after what Lavinia had done to me all those years ago—forcing me to drink from the

Dark Grail to become a slave to the demon Azazel—I was ready to get my revenge.

So I raised the Dark Sword, ran toward her in a blur, and screamed as I speared it through her heart.

Her eyes widened when they met mine.

Blood leaked out of the wound and streamed down her white dress.

Magic stopped flowing out of the Dark Wand, and its crystal dimmed.

I gave the Dark Sword one final twist, then pulled it out of her chest, smiling as she fell back to the ground, dead.

Payback. And damn, it felt good.

The Dark Wand clattered onto the ground next to her, rolled out of her limp hand, and rested on the pavement.

I walked over to Lavinia's body, because even though I knew she was dead, I wanted to make sure. Or maybe I wanted to embrace the glory I felt at finally killing her.

But then, a red glow in the corner of my eye caught my attention.

The Dark Wand.

Its crystal was coming back to life.

No, I thought, and I looked back to Lavinia's body. The Dark Queen of Wands was dead. Stone-cold dead.

This wasn't possible.

I looked back to the Dark Wand, confused when the light in the crystal grew brighter.

Then it levitated in the air, pointed itself toward Torrence, and soared into her waiting palm.

39

TORRENCE

THURSDAY, JUNE 24 (FOUR DAYS AGO)

Magic exploded inside of me, radiating out of my body in the most intense burst of power I'd ever experienced. All of my magic—my purple witch magic, my black mage magic, and my new red magic—wove around themselves and fused together as I became the Dark Queen of Wands.

When the magic settled, I looked around and saw all the others staring at me.

Selena's mouth was wide open.

Sage smirked, then returned to using the Dark Sword to kill any demon nearby.

Reed's dark eyes shined with pride—and love.

But none of them were my concern right now.

Instead, I spun to face Lilith, who looked just as shocked as the others. I pointed the Dark Wand at her and released its magic to create a red barrier dome around her.

I walked toward Raven, and she eyed me warily. She didn't move to attack, although from the way she gripped Excalibur, it was clear she was ready to use it against me at a moment's notice.

I glanced over at where Lilith stood in the boundary dome, her eyes livid as she stared me down, and then I turned my focus back to Raven. "She can't teleport out of that thing," I said. "But I can teleport us in... assuming you want to do the honors?"

A true smile spread across Raven's face as she realized what I was proposing. "You bet I do," she said, and then she took my hand, and I teleported us inside Lilith's prison dome.

40

RAVEN

THURSDAY, JUNE 24 (FOUR DAYS AGO)

Lilith lowered her hand that was holding her sword and dropped it down to her feet, next to the Dark Grail.

She looked pathetic.

Defeated.

"Your army wasn't supposed to have the Golden Scepter," she said.

I thought back to the conversation Annika had had with us a few days ago, when she'd relayed everything she'd learned from the future version of Gemma, and said, "I guess we were one step ahead of you."

"Time travel."

"Yep."

"And now you're here to kill me."

"You bet I am," I said, and victory surged through me, even though I hadn't finished her off yet.

"All right." She squared her shoulders and held my gaze, her red eyes blazing with determination. "We both know you've won. So get it over with. I won't fight back."

I frowned. "That doesn't make it much fun."

Her lips curved up into a small smile. "Are you too much of a Holy Queen to kill someone when they're standing helplessly in front of you?"

I returned her smile, amused that she thought she had a chance to survive this. "I'm not *that* holy," I said, and then I raised Excalibur, ran toward her, and speared the Sword through her heart.

41

BELLA

THURSDAY, JUNE 24 (FOUR DAYS AGO)

THE FEW DEMONS that were still alive turned toward Torrence's boundary dome the moment Raven killed Lilith.

Their eyes flashed red, and they teleported out.

They'd lost. They knew it, and they were running scared.

But it was fine. Because no matter where in the world they'd gone, Avalon's Army would find them and kill them. They didn't stand a chance against us.

Torrence raised the Dark Wand, red magic flowed out of it, and the boundary dome disappeared.

My niece had always been kickass. She reminded me of myself more than her mother—my sister—Amber. Now, with the Dark Wand in her hand and her auburn hair blowing around her, she was an embodiment of magic. Like being the Dark Queen of Wands had always been her destiny.

My focus quickly switched to the Dark Grail sitting beside Lilith's ashes. Because the Dark Grail was pulsing with magic. Like it had a heartbeat.

Its heart was beating at the same time as mine.

An invisible cord of magic connected the Dark Grail to my soul. It was the only thing I saw. The only thing I heard.

The pull toward it consumed me.

Barely aware of what I was doing, I started walking toward it. Its heartbeat grew stronger the closer I got.

"What are you doing?" Raven asked, but I didn't answer her.

Instead, I knelt down, picked up the Dark Grail with both of my hands, and stared down inside of it.

You need to drink, the Grail seemed to speak into my mind.

Drink what? I thought back.

Demon blood.

But the demons are all gone...

"Bella?" Raven said. "Are you okay?"

"The Grail wants me to drink from it," I explained. "It wants me to drink demon blood."

Torrence stepped forward to stand beside Raven,

and her eyes gleamed with excitement. "You're the Dark Queen of Cups," she said.

"Not yet."

Selena teleported to Torrence's side. "What do you mean?"

"Remember how Annika had to drink angel blood to become the Queen of Cups?" I asked, and she nodded, since everyone knew that story. "To complete the transition, I think I might have to do the same—but with demon blood."

"The demons are gone," she said. "They flashed out when Raven killed Lilith. But I can easily do a spell to track one of them down."

"That won't be necessary," someone said from behind me—Sage.

She walked toward me with a short, blonde demon next to her.

On the other side of the demon was Sage's brother, Flint.

Of course. The demon was Flint's mate. Mara. They'd passed Avalon's trials, but after a few years there they chose to live in the Montgomery pack's mansion in Hollywood Hills instead.

When Mara had mated with Flint, their souls had merged. Which meant that unlike all other demons, Mara had a conscience.

As a member of the Montgomery pack, she was the only demon who'd fought alongside Avalon's Army.

"I'll give you my blood," she offered.

I nearly asked if she was sure. But I didn't.

Because becoming the Dark Queen of Cups was my destiny. I needed her blood. And since she was offering, I had no intention of changing her mind.

"Thank you," I said instead.

"It's my pleasure." She stepped forward, held her hand over the Dark Grail, then used her dagger to slice her wrist.

Her blood was so dark that it was nearly black. It dripped out of the wound and pooled at the bottom of the Dark Grail.

Usually, demon blood smelled like smoke and decay.

Mara's blood smelled so sweet that it sang to me, like a siren's song beckoning me closer.

"That's enough," I said.

She pulled her wrist back and placed her other hand over it. A few seconds later, the gash was healed.

Without any further ceremony, I raised the Grail to my lips and drank.

The blood tasted as sweet as it smelled, and the moment I swallowed it, magic surged from my core throughout my body. My skin buzzed, my vision sharpened, and my hearing grew more sensitive. It was like I'd been supercharged with power.

"Your eyes." Raven gasped. "They're red."

"Red's a good color for me," I said with a small smirk.

"So you don't feel… different?"

"My magic is enhanced," I said. "*Way* enhanced. But if you're asking if I've turned evil, then the answer is no. I think I'm like Mara." I glanced at the demon, and she smiled in return. "A demon, but with a conscience. Because I'm the same person as I was before drinking from the Grail. Just more powerful."

"Sort of like me with the Dark Sword," Sage said.

"And me with the Dark Wand," Torrence chimed in.

"Exactly." I was glad that they'd acquired their Dark Objects before me, so I could have them as backup. If I'd been the first, I wasn't sure the others would have accepted me, given that I was now technically part demon.

It didn't feel real.

At the same time, I'd been a dark witch my entire life. I'd never had any issues with controlling my dark magic. If anyone could handle becoming a demon, it was me.

"What can you do with the Dark Grail?" Raven asked.

The answer came to me immediately. "I can bind

people to me, like Lilith did to her," I said. "But don't worry. I'll only do it to people who deserve it."

"And who 'deserves it?'" Selena asked.

"I'd say those demons who teleported out of here with their metaphorical tails behind their legs deserve it first," I said. "I'd love to force them to turn on each other."

"That sounds like a fantastic idea," Torrence said, and the others agreed, too.

"But first, we need to get back to Avalon," Selena said. "I'm sure my mom is dying to know what happened here."

"There is no more Avalon." Mara frowned. "Annika broke her bond with the island when she came here to slay Lucifer."

"She did," I said. "But you've forgotten about the other weapon we have on our side."

"What weapon?"

"Gemma," I said. "Because the Queen of Pentacles had a plan. And if that plan worked, then Avalon should be the same as it was when we left it."

42

MIRA

SUNDAY, JUNE 16, 1912

I WAS HAVING breakfast with Karina in our suite when the familiar feeling of a damp blanket against my skin—the feeling of Lilith's bond—disappeared.

I sucked in a sharp breath as the haze around my brain lifted, and the world grew brighter and more colorful.

Karina placed her teacup down on its saucer and studied me in concern. "What happened?" she asked.

"Lilith's bond," I whispered, as if speaking too loudly would make it return. "It's broken."

"They killed her."

"Yes. That's the only way the bond can break."

Karina's face broke into a smile. "We can finally go home."

I knew she'd be elated. During our time in 1912,

she'd told me all about the love of her life, Peter. Both of them were vampires. Then he'd died in the early twentieth century, and she'd traded her memories of him to a fae to have him brought back from the Beyond. But their love was strong. *Soulmate* strong. As he'd told her stories of their time together, she'd experienced all the feelings she'd felt when those memories had happened. They'd made new memories together. And now they loved each other more than ever.

She couldn't wait to go home to him.

But my thoughts went to William.

I hadn't seen him since the disastrous proposal two weeks ago. He'd sent me a letter a few days later, asking if we could talk, but I didn't reply.

I'd been afraid that if I saw him again, I'd regret refusing to marry him.

Karina had promised me that if I didn't see him, my feelings for him would fade. But they hadn't. Maybe two weeks wasn't long enough for feelings to fade, but somehow, they'd only grown stronger than they'd been before.

And now that it was time to face the fact that I'd never see him again, my heart ached with sorrow.

"You're thinking about William," Karina observed.

"Yes."

"As you should, given that it's time we see him so I can erase his memories of us."

"No." The word came out of my mouth before I could stop it.

She raised an eyebrow. "No?"

"I want to be honest with him."

"You want to tell him that you're a witch with dragon magic who time traveled here from over a hundred years in the future so you could prevent a demon queen from mind controlling you in the present?"

I leveled my gaze with hers, hoping to get across how serious I was about this. "I'm not sure I'll ever be able to live with myself if I don't try," I said.

"He's not going to react well."

"You don't know that."

"Humans rarely react well when they're told about the supernatural world. It's too much for most of their minds to handle."

"William's not 'most people,'" I said in his defense. "He's open-minded. He can handle it."

"And if he can't?"

I held my breath, since I knew what she was getting at.

"If he can't, then you can erase his memories."

She smiled, not even bothering to ask what I wanted

to do if he reacted well. "All right," she said. "Let's change our dresses, and then we'll call on William."

William was out for his morning meal, so Karina and I waited in the reception room of his brownstone for nearly two hours before he returned.

One of the major things I missed from the present day was cell phones.

Karina and I both stood when William entered the reception room.

His soulful eyes immediately locked on mine. "Have you given my proposal more thought?" he asked hopefully.

"I haven't been honest with you," I said, and his brow knitted in confusion. "But I want to change that. Now. And after I'm finished, it may be you who wants to give your proposal more thought. Or revoke it entirely."

"I assure you that nothing you could possibly tell me could change my feelings for you."

"I hope not," I said, and then I took a deep breath, unsure where to start.

I couldn't find the words.

Instead, I reached into the ether and pulled the Dark Crown out of the air.

William's eyes widened. "How did you do that…?" he asked, studying the pocket of air where the Crown had appeared.

I placed the Crown back inside the ether, and he blinked a few times, clearly baffled by what he was seeing. "It was magic," I said simply.

"An illusion," he concluded, and then he chuckled. "Have you come here to tell me that you're part of a traveling circus?"

"It wasn't an illusion," I said. "It was magic. *Real* magic."

"Impossible."

"Remember how we met?" I asked. "When my hat blew into the lens of your camera?"

"Of course." He smiled. "How could I forget the moment when fate blew you my way?"

"Fate didn't blow me your way," I said. "*I* did it. I controlled the wind to make my hat land where it did."

Another emotion crossed over his eyes—concern.

"You believe you controlled the wind?" he asked cautiously.

"I *know* I did." I reached for my air magic, called on the wind, and had it blow around me and William in a circle, like we were standing in the eye of a hurricane.

His eyes widened. "*You're* doing this?"

"Yes." I snapped my fingers, and the wind stopped.

"How?"

"I already told you. Magic."

"So you're saying you're some sort of witch?" He took a step back, looking slightly scared—but also intrigued.

"I have a bit of witch magic." I shrugged. "But that's not how I controlled the wind. You see, on our seventeenth birthday, Gemma, my true sister, and I were gifted with dragon magic—magic that lets us control the elements. I can control air and water. She can control fire and earth. And we can both control time."

He shook his head in disbelief. "I think we should sit down for this," he said, and relief rushed through me, since sitting down was better than him running away or ordering us out of the house.

We both sat, along with Karina, who'd remained silent thus far. I didn't expect her to be any help.

William placed both hands on his knees, sat straight, and faced me. "I understand the four main elements—air, fire, water, and earth," he said, his voice much calmer than I'd expected. "But what do you mean about controlling *time?*"

"I can travel through time," I said, slowly and seriously. "I know you've noticed by now that I'm different than most of the other women around here."

"Because you're from Australia."

"I am," I said. "But that's not why I'm so different. To be honest, I don't even know much about what Australia was like in 1912… because I wasn't born until nearly a century later."

"What are you talking about?"

"I mean I'm not from this time," I said. "I used my magic to travel here from the future."

43

MIRA

SUNDAY, JUNE 16, 1912

I TOLD William everything from the beginning, when Gemma and I had received our magic at the cove.

He received it moderately well. He was stunned, but he didn't kick me out and tell me to never speak to him again, which I took as a good thing.

"Now that the bond to Lilith is broken, it's time for me to go home," I finished.

"To the future," he said hollowly.

"Yes. To the future."

He gazed out the window, looking troubled. Then he snapped his gaze back to mine. "You're able to bring people with you to the future," he said. "I want to go with you."

"You *what?*"

I'd hoped he'd be open-minded, but that was an entirely different level of acceptance.

"I've never felt like I fit in here." He sat forward, his eyes gleaming with excitement. "I've always felt trapped. But if I go with you to your world—to your *time*—I can have a fresh start. With you."

My breath caught in my chest at the possibility. Because that was what I wanted. A life with William.

But as I thought through the logistics, my heart sank.

"The supernatural world is dangerous," I said slowly. "You're human. Even if you came with me to the future, you still wouldn't be part of my world."

"I can go to Avalon." He squared his shoulders with determination. "I'll enter the Angel Trials and become Nephilim."

"You can't be serious," I said, but from the way he was looking at me, it was clear he was. "You found out about the supernatural world a few hours ago. Now you want to become a Nephilim?"

"I want to be with you," he said. "I've known it since the day I met you. I'll do whatever it takes to make that happen. If you want me to, of course."

Karina cleared her throat, and we both looked to her.

I expected her to look appalled. To say no immediately. Instead, she looked interested.

"It's a viable option," she said. "But like Mira said, our world is dangerous—even to the Nephilim."

"You said Lilith was dead," he said.

"The demons aren't the only enemies we've fought, and new enemies will always rise," she explained. "It's simply the way of our world."

"I understand," he said.

She raised an eyebrow. "Do you?"

I said nothing, because Karina was right. There was no way someone could fathom what it was like to fight for your life against terrifying creatures until you had to do it yourself.

"This is my decision," he said, and then he refocused on me. "And yours. If you came here to say goodbye—if you want to return to the future without me—then I understand."

"How are you always so *nice?*" I asked.

"Are the men in your time so terrible?"

I rolled my eyes. "You have no idea."

"Does that mean you'll take me?" He smiled mischievously, like he had a feeling I wanted to say yes.

"What about your family here?" I asked. "And your friends?"

"You're a time traveler. We can come back and visit them whenever we want."

"It wouldn't be that simple," I said. "There are things

to consider—like how quickly we'd age. If we pass the Angel Trials—because remember, I haven't entered them yet, either—we could choose to live on Avalon. If we did that, we'd stop aging in our mid-twenties. Your family would notice it if they're aging and we stay the same."

"And if we don't choose to live on Avalon?" he asked.

"Then we'd age normally."

He paused, thinking. "We could tell my family that we've chosen to start a life for ourselves out west," he said, and then he spoke faster, the way he always did when he was excited about an idea. "They've always known I wasn't happy here, so I doubt it would surprise them. We can visit them occasionally—keeping the time between visits proportional to how much we've aged in the present—and they'd never know the difference."

"Hm," I said. "I suppose that could work."

"Is that a yes?"

I looked to Karina. "What do you think?" I asked.

"I promised you that if William accepted the truth, then how you proceed is up to the two of you," she said. "But even so, it was *always* up to you. You're the Dark Queen of Pentacles. You outrank me."

I wanted to smack myself for not realizing it sooner. Karina was so much older than I was—more than a century older—so it was easy to think she was the one in charge.

But this decision was mine, and *only* mine.

So I looked to William, smiled, and said, "I hope you kept that ring. Because my answer is yes."

44

GEMMA

THURSDAY, JUNE 24 (FOUR DAYS AGO)

I WAS PACING ANXIOUSLY in the house in Norway when Annika appeared in the center of the living room.

She collapsed to the floor, although she still held the Golden Scepter.

I hurried over to her and crouched down to be at her level. "What happened?" I asked. "Did you kill him?"

"I did." She smiled, despite how pale she looked.

"Then why are you so…?"

"Weak?" she finished for me.

"Yeah."

"It's angelic empathy. You know how demons lack a conscience?" she asked, and I nodded. "Angels are the opposite. Our empathy is so strong that we absorb the feelings of everything around us. It's why angels live on

Heaven and don't come to Earth—or to any of the other realms, for that matter. It's too overwhelming to bear."

"It's another reason why you didn't leave Avalon," I realized.

"One of them. But it's going to be okay. Lucifer is dead. Everything is going as planned."

"I hope so." I took a deep breath, since just because Lucifer was dead, it didn't mean everything was okay. "How were the others doing?"

"They were alive when I left," she said, but then her tone darkened. "As were Lilith and Lavinia. I didn't have the strength to remain there after killing Lucifer. The rest is up to the others."

I pressed my lips together and sat back on my heels. Because I could use my key and go to Vegas right now. I could help the others finish off Lilith, Lavinia, and the rest of the demons and dark witches.

But that would involve leaving Annika alone in an incredibly weakened state. And if something happened to Annika, Avalon would be lost forever.

She'd risked so much for us. My duty right now was to her.

"They can handle it," I said. "I know they can."

"I agree." She squared her shoulders, then used the Golden Scepter to help herself stand back up. Color was returning to her face—like the Scepter was giving her strength. "Now, let's get Avalon back."

I took her hand that wasn't holding onto the Scepter. "Do you need time to rest?" I asked.

"No. I've got this."

With that, she teleported us to the middle of a lush jungle in Avalon. Birds chirped, frogs ribbitted in the small pond ahead, and a waterfall roared nearby. What I could make out of the sky above the trees was bright blue with a few puffy white clouds.

Annika looked around in wonder. "It's like I never broke the bond," she said.

"Because you *haven't* broken the bond," I said. "Well, the past version of you hasn't broken the bond. Not yet."

"But she will."

I nodded, since there was always a few second gap between when I time traveled back to the past and when I returned to the future.

That few second gap was why Annika had never time traveled with me before—not even when I'd experimented with my abilities on Avalon. In those few seconds, she wouldn't be on the island, and the bond would break.

Luckily, there was a loophole to this rule. A way to eliminate the few seconds in between leaving and arriving. I'd experienced it the first time I'd traveled back in time.

"You ready?" I asked her, still holding onto her hand.

"I'm ready."

Take us back to the present, I told the Crown, and then we flickered forward in time.

45

GEMMA

TUESDAY, JUNE 29 (PRESENT DAY)

We reappeared in a wasteland.

The trees no longer had leaves. The air was thick with humidity, the sky was a depressing gray, the pond was a thick, muddy mess, and silence hung heavy around us.

Avalon was dead.

And then, new memories flooded my mind.

They started eight days ago, when Annika had received a fire message while training us and disappeared. When she'd come back, she'd said that Jacen had needed to speak with her, and had left it at that.

After training, she'd asked me to accompany her to her quarters. She told me she'd been visited by a future version of myself, and then told me everything the version of me from the future had told her.

From there, we'd gathered all the leaders of Avalon around the round table and filled them in. They'd been horrified to hear about Lucifer and how they'd died in the original version of the battle, but they were as determined as we were to change the outcome.

Four days later, when it was time to go to the Vegas Strip, we were ready.

It had killed me to say goodbye to everyone—especially to Ethan. But he'd promised me that things would be different this time around, and I'd believed him.

It took all my willpower not to go with them. But trusting the future version of myself was our best chance of getting everything right this time.

Annika and I had waited anxiously on Avalon as they'd fought.

Then, hours later, they'd returned. *All* of them. Ethan had wrapped me in a hug so tight it felt like he was going to break me.

The only person noticeably missing was Mira.

But I'd told myself that it was okay. She and I hadn't had much time to talk on the Titanic. For all I knew, the version of her I'd seen there had come from further in the future.

I'd simply need to be patient. And when everything was over, if I still hadn't heard from her, I could try to find her in 1912. I didn't want to have to do that, since I didn't want to risk changing anything else in the past, but it was still an option.

In the days that had followed, the Nephilim Army had tracked down the demons that had deserted the battle and killed them all.

We'd beaten them.

All of them.

Annika pressed her fingers to her temples, and she beamed as the memories of the new timeline filled her mind, too. "We won," she said, and she pulled me into a tight hug. "After all these years, it's finally over."

Finally, she loosened her arms around me and looked around the dead forest, frowning.

"This is what it looked like when I first got here all those years ago," she said.

"I remember," I said, since I'd traveled back in time to see Avalon before Annika had arrived. "So, are you ready to bring life back to Avalon—again?"

"You bet I am."

Take us back five minutes, I thought to the Crown.

We flickered for a few seconds, and then Avalon was back to its typical lively state.

"Amazing," Annika said as she looked around.

"It is," I agreed.

The only way Avalon could be alive like this was if

our past selves—at least the past version of *Annika*—had remained on the island.

That was the loophole. Since there'd only been one version of each of us in existence for the past four days, I was still able to travel us back to any time in that window.

I'd chosen to take us back five minutes, because this time, I wasn't going to time travel us back to the present. That few second gap without Annika on Avalon wouldn't exist, because we were going to catch up with the present naturally.

Annika paced around in front of the pond. "How much longer?" she asked.

"About two minutes," I replied, because ever since receiving my time travel magic, I had a natural feel for time in general.

She continued to pace silently as we waited.

Two minutes later, Avalon was still intact.

"Okay," I said, and Annika stopped pacing. "We did it."

"Just like that?" she asked.

"The hope was that no change would happen," I said. "So, yes. Just like that."

"And our counterparts…?"

"They're gone," I said, since that was what had happened to my counterpart the first time I'd time traveled in the Seventh Kingdom. "We're the only versions of ourselves that exist right now."

"So, wherever we were, we disappeared."

"Yep. Which means it's time for you to teleport us back to the castle, so we can fill everyone in."

"It's a good thing we already prepped them," she said with a relieved smile. "Otherwise, I can't imagine how we'd begin to explain."

"Tell me about it," I said. "I sometimes even have a hard time wrapping my mind around it myself. But it worked. And in the end, that's what matters."

"It worked," she repeated, and her eyes filled with tears. "Avalon is still alive. Because of you."

"Because of all of us," I corrected her, and then I walked forward, took her hands, and she teleported us to the castle.

46

GEMMA

TUESDAY, JUNE 29 (PRESENT DAY)

Jacen was waiting in the living area of his and Annika's quarters when we popped in.

He tilted his head, his brow scrunched. "That's strange. I was just talking to you, but..." he trailed off, clearly confused.

"But what?" I asked.

"Nothing," he said, and he snapped back to focus.

"Wrong," Annika said, and she ran up to him and pulled him in for a kiss.

I averted my eyes, not wanting to intrude any more than I already had on their private moment.

"So much has happened," she said, and figuring it was safe, I looked back over to them again.

He stared down at her with complete love and

adoration. "Does that mean it worked?" he asked with a smile.

Before either of us could confirm, there was a loud knock on the door. I glanced at Annika, since it was up to her to decide who to let into her quarters.

She walked over to the door and opened it.

Torrence stormed inside, holding the Dark Wand. Its red crystal was glowing like crazy.

I knew from my memories of the new timeline that Torrence was now the Dark Queen of Wands. But seeing her in all her glory—and feeling the insane amount of magic that emanated off her—was a totally different story.

She faced me, her eyes a storm of confusion. "I was enjoying some much-needed private time with Reed when I suddenly remembered you and I going back to Pompeii, getting the Golden Scepter from an angel, and you making an entire *volcano* erupt so we could do so," she said, the air around her humming with magic. "But that definitely didn't happen. And at the same time, it did." She crossed her arms the best she could, given that she was holding the Dark Wand. "Explain."

"You remembered it because it happened," I said simply. "We needed to go back in time to find the Golden Scepter because—"

"Because it's the only weapon that can kill Lucifer,"

she said. "We talked about it in Pompeii. We talked about the battle as if we'd lost it. Except we didn't lose. We *won*."

"I didn't think you'd remember all of that," I said. "It must be because you were there with me. It's the only thing I can think of to explain it."

"It's the only thing that explains *what?*"

I wracked my mind for where to start.

"You weren't a member of the council before the battle, so you don't know the plan we had going into it," I said. "It involved time travel."

"I figured as much." She rolled her eyes.

"I'm trying to explain," I said patiently, since I knew this had to be a lot for her to process.

"Okay." She huffed, and the red crystal on the Dark Wand dimmed, which I took to mean that she was getting a handle on her emotions. "Go ahead."

I nodded, then continued, "You remember one battle, right? The one where we beat Lucifer and Lilith and Lavinia?"

"Yes."

"Like I was saying before, that wasn't the first time the final battle played out," I said. "Because there was another time. A time when we lost."

I waited a few seconds for it to sink in.

"You changed it," she realized. "You went back in time and made sure we won."

"*We* went back in time and made sure we won," I said, and then I filled her in on everything that had happened before our mission to get the Golden Scepter in Pompeii.

47

GEMMA

WEDNESDAY, JUNE 30 (PRESENT DAY)

THE MAJORITY of yesterday was spent with the council, filling them in on everything that had happened.

Last night was dedicated to Ethan.

I'd never be able to forget seeing him killed in the original battle, and I was going to appreciate every moment I had with him.

We were woken that morning by a loud knock on the door.

I covered our heads with the comforter, but whoever was knocking was insistent. Once it was clear they weren't going to give up, I sat up and let out a frustrated breath.

"Give us a minute!" I said, and then Ethan and I scurried out of bed and quickly got dressed.

I opened the door and found Skylar standing on the other side.

She looked back at Ethan—who was doing his best to hide his annoyance at being woken up—then cleared her throat. "Sorry for the disturbance, but both of you need to come to the dock," she said. "Someone's about to arrive who I know you'll want to see."

"Mira," I said hopefully, and Skylar didn't confirm or deny. She simply moved to the side so Ethan and I could head out of our quarters.

I hurried through the hall and down the steps to the cavern below the castle so quickly that I nearly stumbled over my feet on the way there.

Annika and Jacen were already waiting at the dock, staring out at the still water in the underground lake.

"It's going to be Mira," I said, as if saying it could make it true.

Annika stepped toward me, squeezed my hand, and gave me a small smile. "I hope so."

Finally, after what felt like an hour but what was really only three minutes, a boat turned around the corner.

My heart dropped at the sight of a man I didn't recognize, who was wearing clothes that looked like they'd come out of the early twentieth century. He was gazing around in wonder, like he was seeing the world for the first time. I sniffed to try to pick up his supernatural scent, but he was either wearing a cloaking ring, or he was human.

Why did Skylar wake me up for *this?*

But then, another boat turned around the corner.

Mira.

Her eyes locked with mine, and she stood up in her boat, waving in excitement. She was beaming in a way that I hadn't seen since before we'd gotten our magic, and I knew in that moment that my bubbly, fun, mischievous twin sister was *back.*

I stood on the balls of my feet, barely able to stand still as I waited for her boat to land at the dock.

The crystals of the Dark Crown glimmered as the fire from the torches reflected off them. Mira was also dressed like she'd come from the twentieth century, and I realized that she must not have bothered changing after returning from 1912.

The man's boat reached the dock first, and Mira's followed a few seconds later.

Before I could process that she was truly *here,* Mira bounded off the boat, landed gracefully on the dock, and pulled me in for a huge hug.

I hugged her back tightly, as if afraid she could disappear at any moment.

Eventually we forced ourselves apart.

The moment we did, the man who'd come with her stepped to her side and took her left hand.

Her hand with a *ring* on her finger.

Mira never wore rings on her left hand. She'd always said those fingers were staying bare until she was engaged.

I yanked her hand out of his, and my mouth dropped open at the sight of the massive diamond ring.

"Please tell me this isn't what I think it is," I said.

"You mean an engagement ring?"

"Yeah. That."

She smiled playfully. "So you want me to lie to you?"

"We're *seventeen*," I said. "You can't get engaged at seventeen."

But at the same time, it wasn't the worst thing in the world. Because if Mira had accepted a proposal from whoever this guy was—and, to give her credit, he *was* very attractive—then it meant she was over Ethan.

In fact, she'd barely glanced at Ethan since arriving to Avalon.

"Things are different in 1912," she said.

"You were there for a few *weeks*," I said. "It's not like you're from there. Unless you're planning on going back?"

Sparks of fire buzzed around my fingers at the possibility. Because I'd finally gotten my sister back. She couldn't just leave to go off and live at the turn of the twentieth century with a man she'd met a few weeks ago.

Well, technically she can, I reminded myself.

And would that be the worst thing in the world? If that was what she'd decided would make her happy—and if she'd come all the way to Avalon to tell me—then I'd support her. Besides, I could time travel, too. I could visit her there whenever I wanted.

"Chill." She chuckled, as if she could read my racing thoughts. "I'm staying here. *William* and I are staying here."

I turned to *William* and studied him. He looked only a few years older than us, and his sandy blond hair had gotten ruffled up from the trip to Avalon. If he wasn't dressed in aristocratic clothes, I would have thought he was a bohemian artist.

"It's a pleasure to meet you," he said, holding out his hand for me to shake.

I did, although I was stunned the entire time.

When I let go, my hand immediately found Ethan's.

"I guess Mira told you about… us?" I asked William.

"You mean how she's a witch with dragon elemental magic, and that she traveled more than a century back in the past to wait for you to kill Lilith in the present?"

"All right," I said, surprised by how calmly he'd said it all. "I'll take that as a yes."

He stood straighter and smiled, like he'd aced an exam.

I looked back and forth between the two of them, as if doing so could answer my questions. From the way they were angled toward each other, I could practically feel their love oozing in the air between them.

Annika took a step toward Mira. "Welcome to Avalon," she said with a warm smile. "I'm Annika—the Earth Angel. I'm so glad you made it here safely."

"Trust me—so am I," Mira said.

"Normally we start with orientation…" Annika said, although from the way she trailed off, I could tell she knew that orientation was going to have to wait.

"Do you mind if Mira and I go to my quarters first?" I asked, even though as a Queen, I didn't have to ask for permission to do anything. "So we can catch up alone?"

"Your 'quarters?'" Mira asked, raising an eyebrow.

I supposed it did sound pretty fancy when it was put that way.

"Come and see," I said, and I reached for her hand, leading her toward the stairs. "Because I know you're gonna *love* it here."

48

GEMMA

THURSDAY, JULY 1 (PRESENT DAY)

THE NEXT DAY, Ethan called a council meeting.

It was tight around the table with the new Dark Queens and their partners, but we managed to squeeze enough chairs together. Once everyone was situated, they looked to Ethan, curious about what he wanted to discuss.

I, of course, already knew. Because we'd gone to the Eternal Library last night, and Hecate had given us the final piece of information we needed to do what needed to be done.

Now, we needed to get the others on board to help us.

"As the king of Ember, I have a duty to my people," Ethan started, the confidence in his voice making him *sound* like a king. "Long ago, the dragons lived in peace in our native realm. Then the mages and fae declared Ember a 'prison realm,' and they started sending their worst criminals there."

The others nodded, since this was common knowledge.

"The dark mages and fae—a group that now calls themselves the Dark Allies—took over Ember and turned the majority of my people into slaves," he continued. "The dragons who are free are deep in hiding, but they can't remain that way forever. The Dark Allies must be stopped so we can reclaim our realm."

Everyone was silent as they processed the fact that Ethan was ready to jump into another war so soon after we'd won the war against the demons.

"I assume you have a plan?" Raven finally asked.

"The dragons are strong," Ethan said. "The only reason why they can't fight back against the Dark Allies is because the Dark Allies keep their magic bound with cuffs. These cuffs were created by one of the first dark mages sent to Ember—the Supreme Mage, King Ragnorr. If we kill King Ragnorr, the cuffs will deactivate, and the dragons will be able to use their magic to stand up against the Dark Allies."

"I have no doubt that the dragons are strong," Julian said. "But the Supreme Mages are immortal *and* indestructible. They can't be killed."

"Wrong," Ethan said. "A Supreme Mage can be killed by someone with more magic than they have. In King Ragnorr's case, since he practices dark magic, he can only be killed by someone with more dark magic than he possesses."

That was what we'd learned from Hecate last night. And, after sharing it with the group, Ethan's gaze immediately landed on Torrence's.

She stared back at him, her expression giving away nothing.

"As the Dark Queen of Wands, you're the only person on Earth with more dark magic than King Ragnorr," he said to her. "To free the dragons, I need your help."

Reed moved protectively closer to Torrence. "Even if you succeed, the mages and fae will continue to send their prisoners to Ember," he said to Ethan. "What will stop them from overtaking the dragons again?"

"Ember never belonged to the mages and the fae," he said. "They had no right to turn it into a place to dump their prisoners."

Reed smirked, amused. "You think the mages will stop sending their prisoners to Ember because you asked them nicely?"

"I think we have a lot of powerful people sitting around this table, and that if we approach the fae and the mages, we can come up with another solution. One that *doesn't* involve them dumping all their criminals into a realm with an innocent supernatural species."

"A realm like Hell?" Bella asked.

"Yes," Ethan said. "That would work nicely."

"We just defeated the demons," Annika broke in. "Now you want to open a portal to Hell and risk them escaping again?"

"The portals that currently lead the fae and mages to Ember are one-way," he said calmly. "The Dark Allies have more magic than the demons. If they couldn't break through the portals to escape Ember, then the demons won't be able to break through them to escape Hell."

"And who's going to create these portals?"

This was where the question I'd asked Hecate last night came in handy.

"One-way portals like the ones leading to Ember are nearly impossible to create or destroy," I said. "But if the Holy and Dark Queens of Wands work together, they'll be able to do it."

"How do you know?" she asked.

"Through the same source that told me the Golden Scepter was the only object in existence that could kill Lucifer."

I tensed, expecting her to demand me to explain further.

She didn't. Instead, she gave me a single nod, showing me that she was taking my word as the truth.

"I can talk to Sorcha," Selena volunteered. "Given that Lilith unleashed the plague on the Otherworld that killed a huge amount of fae, I'm sure she'll delight in the idea of throwing our criminals into Hell instead of Ember."

"And the mages?" Annika asked.

"Sorcha is close with our king," Reed said. "If she proposes the idea to him, I'm sure he'll listen."

He said it with so much confidence that no one questioned him.

"But there's still one important factor," he continued. "You said you needed Torrence to kill King Ragnorr." He turned to look at her. "Is this something you're willing to do?"

Her grip around the Dark Wand tightened. "If it wasn't for Gemma and Ethan, then I'd still be fully dark, I'd still be locked in Ember, and Selena would still be dead," she said. "So you bet I want to help." With that, she turned to me and asked, "When do we leave? And what's the plan?"

"I already have a plan," I said. "I can share it now. As for when we leave..." I trailed off and looked to Annika.

Even though all the Queens were technically equal, it always felt like she was the leader.

"We have much to discuss with the fae and the mages," she said. "We can start working on that immediately. Then, once we come to an agreement, you can do whatever you need to do to free the dragons and give them back their home."

49

TORRENCE

FRIDAY, JULY 9 (PRESENT DAY)

It took Sorcha a week to convince the mages that if we succeeded in overthrowing the Dark Allies, they'd agree to send their criminals to Hell instead of Ember. During that time, the council brainstormed to perfect Gemma's plan.

It involved time travel.

Of *course* it involved time travel.

Understanding time travel was eventually going to be the death of me. Time was supposed to move *forward*—not in every which way and other timelines/universes that Gemma created. But I had my role, and I was ready to play it.

Now, it was just me, Sorcha, and Reed standing in the mausoleum-like thing in the palace of the Otherworld, looking down into the red portal that led to

Ember. I held the Dark Wand in my right hand, and the crystal glowed brightly.

Reed placed his hand on my shoulder, and when I looked up at him, he was concerned. "Are you sure you can control it?" he asked.

"I can," I promised. "All it takes is remembering the devastated look on your face when we were prisoners in the mages' dungeon, when I lied and told you I didn't love you."

A shadow crossed over his eyes. "In that moment, it wasn't a lie."

"It was the darkness talking," I said, since back then, I'd been consumed by it. "But you knew I loved you, even though the dark magic was smothering my emotions. Now, I want to be able to give you my heart— all of it. My love for you is what keeps the darkness under control."

"You keep your magic under control," he said.

"Maybe. But you make a fantastic incentive."

He smirked, then pulled me close and kissed me. His kiss was hard and rough, but somehow sweet at the same time, which was pretty much Reed in a nutshell.

I would have stripped off his clothes and made love to him right there if Sorcha didn't clear her throat, interrupting our moment.

So I pulled away from Reed, my cheeks flushed from kissing him.

His dark eyes swirled with intensity, like he was hypnotized by me.

"We'll continue this later," I promised. "After I'm back from Ember."

"Come back safely," he said. "Swear to me that you will."

"I swear it."

The Wand's red crystal glowed after I said it, as if confirming my promise.

"Good," he said. "I'll see you soon."

"See you soon," I said, and then I looked back down into the portal.

Like the one in the mage realm—Mystica—the stones built up in a circle around it made it resemble a well. A *deep* well, seeing as there was no bottom in sight.

But luckily, since I'd been down a similar portal before, I knew what to expect. So, not wanting to drag out this farewell any longer than necessary, I stepped onto the ledge of the stones and jumped into Ember.

50

TORRENCE

FRIDAY, JULY 9 (PRESENT DAY)

I LANDED ON MY FEET, my knees bent to absorb the fall, with one hand touching the ground to brace myself and the other holding firmly onto the Dark Wand. I was in the middle of a desert, and the only things breaking up the landscape were the boulders scattered throughout the area. It was bright outside, and the hot sun scorched my skin.

When I righted myself, I made sure the Wand's crystal was glowing brightly, and that black, dark magic covered my eyes.

It didn't take me long to spot the two groups nearby —the dark mages and the dark fae. The fae had wings of all different colors, and the mages wore robes that made them look like Jedi apprentices. Although, given the circumstances, they would most definitely be *Sith* apprentices. Except they wouldn't be apprentices. Because all the mages and fae in Ember were powerful enough to be sent to a one-way prison realm.

The groups stood at opposite sides of the landing spot, and all of them eyed me warily.

A representative of the mages stepped forward. I couldn't see his hair color under his robes, but his eyes were a startling pale blue.

"On behalf of the Dark Allies, welcome to Ember," he said. "I sense strong magic in you."

"You better," I said with a confident smirk. "Because I'm the Dark Queen of Wands. And I'm here to take my rightful place beside your king."

He pressed his lips together, silent.

I bet he hadn't expected *that* one.

"Are you referring to King Ragnorr?" he finally asked.

"Of course I am." I narrowed my eyes. "What other king of our people would I be referring to?"

He sized me up, and another mage stepped up next to him—a female with eyes the same color as his. "King Ragnorr has made no mention of a bride," she said calmly, although I could tell by how tensed she was that she was defensive, and probably a little scared.

"What can I say?" I chuckled, like this didn't concern me. "I like surprises."

Then, someone spoke up from behind me. "Your weapon looks like the Holy Wand of legend," she said, and I glanced over my shoulder to see a fae girl with pale skin and even paler blonde hair. She held her chin high, as if she thought she was better than me.

I spun around to face her. "The Holy Wand has blue crystals—not red," I said. "This is the Dark Wand. And it chose me as its Queen. Which makes me one of the most powerful mages in the world."

"If that's true, then why are you here?"

"What do you mean—*why am I here?*" When I imitated her, I made her nasally voice sound even more annoying than it already was.

"I mean that if you're as powerful as you say you are, how did you get captured and sent here? Shouldn't you have been able to use your magic as the 'Dark Queen of Wands' to avoid being banished in the first place?"

The way she said my title—as if it were a joke—*really* pissed me off.

"She has a good point," the mage with pale blue eyes asked. "If you are who you say you are, and if you've truly been chosen by the Dark Wand, then prove it."

"Fine," I snarled, faced the group of dark fae, and called on my magic.

I blasted it out of the crystal at them like a red laser beam, cutting through their bodies in a straight line.

Some of their mouths were still open in shock when the top halves of their bodies tumbled to the ground next to their already collapsed bottom halves.

All of them dead.

Murdered.

By me.

Disgust rolled through me. Because even though they were criminals, you never knew someone's life story. Maybe some of them had been sent to Ember unjustifiably. Maybe they were just doing their jobs of guarding the portal after Gemma, Mira, Ethan, Reed, and I killed the previous group of guards.

But this was war, and the dragons needed their home realm back. I was their best chance at making that happen. To do that, I had to convince the dark mages that this wasn't an act.

If that meant embracing more of my dark side, then so be it. I trusted myself to rein it in later.

So I inhaled the roasted smell of death, plastered a chilling smile on my face, and spun around to face the dark mages. "Is that enough proof for you?" I asked so sweetly that it was like honey dripping from my voice.

The female dark mage held her gaze with mine. "The fae will be angry with you for killing their guards."

"I'm a mage," I said. "I don't care about the fae."

"We don't care about the fae, either," she replied. "But they're our allies. So we tolerate them."

My magic crashed around like a tsunami of frustration inside of me, and the Wand's crystal glowed red again.

I had to take a few deep breaths to stop myself from doing to the dark mages what I'd just done to the dark fae.

They were so silent that I could practically smell their fear.

It was time to take advantage of that.

Time to let them know that *they* served *me*.

"What part of 'take me to your king' don't you understand?" My voice sliced through the air as sharply as the glass I wanted to pierce through their souls.

I could have sworn I saw the man quiver. "We can't leave the portal unmanned," he finally said. "But my sister will escort you to our palace, and there, she'll present you to our king."

51

TORRENCE

FRIDAY, JULY 9 (PRESENT DAY)

The brother and sister duo didn't bother to introduce themselves before walking toward me.

Once they were close enough, the woman held out her hand. She was only a few years older than I was.

I glanced at her hand skeptically.

She continued to hold my gaze, showing no ounce of fear. "If you want us to trust you, then you need to trust us," she said firmly.

"Fine," I said. "But if you take me anywhere other than your palace, I'll take care of you like I did those fae. Except unlike I did for them, I'll make sure to take my time while killing you."

She didn't so much as flinch. "You asked us to take you to the king," she said. "I'm offering to do that. You can either accept or not. Your choice."

I contemplated trying to force her into a blood oath. But no—this show of faith would be good.

It would make them think I was truly on their side.

Anyway, if she took me somewhere else, I'd follow through on that promise I'd made her, then return here to show her body as proof that I should be taken seriously, and get another dark mage to do as I'd asked.

"I accept," I said, and then I lowered my hand into her waiting palm.

She flashed us out of there in an instant.

We appeared on the top of a hill that overlooked what I assumed was the sprawling dark mage kingdom. It reminded me of the one from *Frozen*—not the ice palace Elsa had created, but the one in Arendelle where she'd lived with her sister.

Tall stone walls surrounded it like a fortress.

"There's a boundary spell around the kingdom that makes it so no one can teleport directly inside," the dark mage explained, which didn't surprise me, since all the kingdoms on Earth were protected by similar barriers. "We'll have to walk from here."

"Sounds reasonable," I said, continuing before she could walk forward. "Also, I don't know your name."

"That's because I didn't give it." Darkness swirled in her eyes again, but a second before that, I'd seen something I recognized greatly—because it had been the way

Gemma had looked at Mira when she'd believed Mira and Ethan were a couple.

Jealousy.

"Do you want King Ragnorr for yourself?" I asked her.

"Of course not," she said, and she motioned to her left ring finger, which had a diamond band around it. She was married. "That Wand, on the other hand..." Her gaze traveled to the Dark Wand gripped firmly in my hand.

"You want power."

"I'm a dark mage," she said. "Of course I want power."

"Then after you take me to the king, I'll ensure you're rewarded," I said. "But to do that, I need your name."

"Freya Kristiansen," she said, and then she looked at me for my response. When I didn't give her one, she asked, "And what's yours?"

"I'm the Dark Queen of Wands," I said simply, and then I looked back to the palace. "Now, let's proceed."

She nodded, and I followed her down the path that led to the stone wall.

The guard at the tall wooden door immediately focused on the Wand. Then he got ahold of himself and looked to Freya. "A new recruit?" he asked.

"This one is special," Freya said, although she didn't

elaborate further. "We need escorts to the palace—and an immediate audience with the king."

52

TORRENCE

FRIDAY, JULY 9 (PRESENT DAY)

Freya must have held authority in the dark mage kingdom, because the guard quickly gathered an entourage that marched me to the palace.

Along the way, I spotted servants dressed in rags working along the sides of the streets. Their wrists were cuffed, just like mine had been when my magic had been bound.

Dragons.

They barely paid me any attention as I walked by. It was like their souls had been shattered after years—or likely lifetimes—of slavery.

Eventually, we reached the wide steps that led to the giant front doors of the palace and marched inside.

The interiors of the palace had large rooms, but the decorations were sparser than I'd expected. Most everything was made of some variation of brown stone, which I supposed was because there weren't many other resources in Ember's desert environment to work with. There wasn't much natural light in the palace, either. I felt like I was walking into a giant crypt.

A long hallway led to a giant room where a man wearing a black robe and an obsidian crown sat on a stone throne. He looked to be about twenty-five years old, but his hard, strong features made it clear that he was far, far older than that.

And then there were his eyes. Pitch black, as if permanently consumed by dark magic. There was something so terrifying in them that it made me want to look anywhere else but his eyes, but I stood strong, not wanting to show any signs of weakness.

But even though I kept my gaze on his, I'd already seen the dark mages and dragon slaves along the sides of the room. I wondered why he kept the slaves in there—surely there was nothing they could do for him in the throne room.

Then I realized: they were a display of the power he held over them. He was showing them off as if they were pieces in a museum.

He glanced lazily at the Wand in my hand, unfazed. He'd flicked his eyes so quickly that it was like he couldn't be bothered to move.

Clearly this was a man who'd grown so used to power that he believed himself invincible.

"Who are you?" he asked, sounding bored and annoyed.

"I'm Torrence Devereux—the Dark Queen of Wands," I said. "And I've come here for you."

Before he had a chance to realize what was happening, I raised my Wand and shot a burst of red magic through the crystal. At the same time as my magic fried him to smithereens, I created a boundary dome around myself strong enough to ward off any possible attacks by the other dark mages in the room.

Turned out that it hadn't been necessary, because all of the dark mages were staring in shock at King Ragnorr's charred bones, which were now in piles on the seat of the throne and the floor.

The cuffs around the dragons' wrists clattered to the floor, too. Many of them held out their hands in wonder, and life started appearing in their previously sallow features.

I held the Dark Wand up victoriously. "I've freed you from the dark mages," I said, my voice echoing in the cavernous room. "Now, it's time for you to *fight!*"

Fire, ice, stone, and air launched out of the dragons' hands, and then I flashed out.

I reappeared in the underwater dragon kingdom, in the room on the top of the tower where I'd first met the Elders.

Darius and Hypatia were waiting there—along with Ethan, Gemma, Mira, and Selena.

"He's dead," I said. "And it was *easy*. He was so arrogant that he wasn't even on guard for an attack."

"Or you're so strong that he never stood a chance against you," Selena said.

"Maybe."

"Wow." Her lips formed into an O of disbelief. "Are you actually being *modest?*"

"Of course not," I said, since "modest" wasn't a thing I did. "You should have seen him. He truly believed nothing could touch him. And then I turned him into a pile of bones—on his own throne."

"Nice." Ethan nodded in approval. "I want to hear all about it later. But now, let's move on to part two."

53

GEMMA

THURSDAY, JULY 8 (YESTERDAY)

I HELD Ethan's hands and flickered us one day into the past.

Mira appeared next to us with Selena.

We were in the same place we'd been standing before—in the center of the meeting room on the top floor of the tower. Hypatia and Darius were waiting for us there, looking at us expectantly.

"The plan worked," Ethan told them. "At 3pm tomorrow, Torrence will kill King Ragnorr and free the dragons."

"Incredible." Hypatia grinned.

"Truly." Darius looked to Mira, and then to me. "Your abilities add an entirely new level to battle strategy."

"I'm glad to help free the dragons," I said. "But the

real hero is Torrence. She's the one who killed King Ragnorr."

"There are no 'real' heroes," Hypatia said kindly. "There are simply heroes, and I'd say all of you are ones."

I glanced down for a second, because even now, I wasn't the best at receiving compliments.

"While I agree with Hypatia, let's save the congratulations for later," Darius said. "Because this isn't over yet.

"No, it's not," I agreed, and then I walked over to the table, where a piece of paper and a pen were waiting for me.

It worked, I wrote. *And we're on our way to help.*

54

GEMMA

FRIDAY, JULY 9 (PRESENT DAY)

After leaving Torrence the note, the four of us didn't return to the present. Instead, we remained there and helped the Elders prepare the dragons in the kingdom for what was coming next. They'd already been told the plan, but a new sense of hope arose after they learned that Torrence had successfully killed King Ragnorr.

Now, Ethan was flying through the sky in dragon form, and I sat on his back, my hands wrapped around the spikes coming up out of the bottom of his neck. Although I didn't need to hold on as much as I thought I would, since thanks to our twin flame bond, I could feel what movements he was going to make at nearly the same time as he made them. With Ethan, flying felt natural—which said a lot, given that air wasn't one of my elements.

Half of the dragons from the kingdom flew behind us—nearly six hundred in total.

The other half were with Mira and Selena.

The dark mage kingdom finally came into view, and at the exact time Torrence had said it would, the roof of the palace exploded in a flash of red light.

Dragons flew out from the top—more and more of them, far more than were behind us. There were so many dragons that they covered the sky, blotting out the sun so it seemed like night.

Just when I thought there couldn't be any more dragons inside, Torrence rode up on the back of one, her hair flying wildly around her, and her eyes immediately locked on mine.

"There are only dark mages left inside," she said. "Time to burn them down."

All at once, the fire dragons released fire from their mouths—Ethan at the head of the group.

The palace exploded in flames.

As it did, more and more dragons flew up from the rest of the kingdom.

Terrified dark mages ran through the streets, their eyes black with rage as they released clouds of black death magic from their hands. Their dark magic *did* hit some dragons, and I winced as I watched the dragons' bodies fall to the ground and shift back into human form.

But for the most part, the dragons soared over the mages, fueled by their anger as they killed them with ice and fire. Mages flooded past the stone wall surrounding the kingdom and tried to make their way toward the desert, but they were killed, too.

The world burned as much as it had when Vesuvius had exploded over Pompeii, and the air smelled like cooked flesh. The mages continued to try to attack with their magic, but from their terrified screams and continued attempts to flee, they knew they'd lost.

It wasn't even thirty minutes before the entire kingdom was up in flames.

No wonder the mages had insisted on binding the dragons' magic. There were so many dragons in Ember that they didn't have a chance against them otherwise.

Even crazier was that dragons naturally had a peaceful nature. They didn't attack unless provoked. They were content in Ember, and had no interest in conquering other realms. They probably would have lived peacefully alongside the Dark Allies if the Dark Allies hadn't made them their enemies.

Once there was nothing left of the kingdom but ash,

Ethan led the hoard of dragons to the portals that dropped people off from the Otherworld and Mystica.

As we got closer, so did another group of dragons opposite us, with Mira and Selena in the front.

Ethan lowered himself to the ground, and I hopped off his back before he returned to human form. The dragons that Torrence, Selena, and Mira were riding did the same, and the other dragons followed suit.

There were so many people in all directions that I couldn't comprehend the size of the crowd. Most of them were dressed in the simple, worn clothes of slaves, and they looked bewildered, as if they weren't sure if this was a dream or reality.

"How'd it go with the dark fae?" Torrence asked Selena.

"Burned them to the ground," she said, and thunder rumbled through the sky, followed with flashes of lightning.

The dragons looked up in amazement, as if the lightning was a blessing from the Heavens.

"Same with the dark mages," Torrence said, and then they aimed their Wands upward and created a sort of magical television screen high enough in the sky that everyone in the crowd could see it. They also created small glowing orbs that buzzed around us like cameras to show us on the screens.

The sight of it silenced the dragons even more.

Ethan faced the orb closest to him, and his face filled the screen. "Ember is ours again," he said, and the crowd erupted into cheers and applause.

He let them cheer for about twenty seconds. Then he held a hand up, and they silenced.

"It's thanks to the most powerful mage and the most powerful fae in the universe that your freedom was given to you today," he said. "And they're going to make sure the dark mages and fae can never come here again."

The orbs focused on Torrence and Selena, and the two of them turned toward the red portal. They held their Wands up toward it, nodded at each other, then shot their magic out toward it.

Red and blue magic collided with the portal, zapping it out of existence.

They made it look so *easy*.

The dragons seemed to agree, given the shocked looks on their faces.

"Rebuilding will take time," Ethan said. "But we lived off the land in the beginning, and for now, we'll do it once more. And as your king, I promise that Ember will never be taken from us again."

More cheers, and again, Ethan held his hand up to silence them.

"I'm happy to announce that I won't be the only one

who will help pave our way into a new Golden Age," he said. "Because we wouldn't be here today without help from my twin flame, Gemma Brown. And it's my honor to introduce her to you as my queen."

I held my breath, since this was the part I was most nervous about. Because unlike Ethan, I wasn't a full dragon. Yes, I was gifted with dragon magic, but I couldn't shift.

I wasn't truly one of them.

Would they accept me as their queen?

Luckily, I didn't have to worry about it for long.

Because the moment I appeared on the screen, and Ethan clasped his hand around mine, the crowd once again erupted into approving applause.

I relaxed, but only slightly. Because it didn't end here. There was still a kingdom to rebuild.

But the dragons believed in Ethan, and *I* believed in Ethan.

It was going to take work. But like he'd promised our people, I trusted that we'd lead Ember into a new Golden Age—together.

55

GEMMA

WEDNESDAY, JULY 14 (PRESENT DAY)

THANKS TO HECATE'S keys and the tokens we'd used the first time we'd come to Ember, I was able to return to Earth with Mira, Torrence, and Selena.

Ethan was staying in Ember, because they needed him to lead as king. As his queen, I was going to join him soon, although I did plan to use my key to visit my family on Earth as much as possible. Especially because along with being the queen of Ember, I was also the Queen of Pentacles, which meant I had responsibilities to Earth and Avalon, too.

There was so much for me to do in the future.

But first, I had to say goodbye to my past.

Which was why I was currently in my room above the café, going through my stuff to decide what I wanted to take with me to Avalon and what I wanted to keep around for when I visited Mom. My books were obviously in the box labeled "Avalon," and now I was sorting through my clothes.

I reached for a sweatshirt—one with my high school's name on it—unfolded it, and froze when I saw the name on the front.

Ocean Park High.

No. That wasn't right. I'd never heard of a school called Ocean Park High.

Except as I continued to look at the sweatshirt, new memories layered over the old ones.

Ocean Park High was the name of my school.

Still holding onto the sweatshirt, I hurried into Mira's room. Mom was in there with her, helping her decide what shoes she wanted to take to Avalon, and which ones she wanted to leave here.

I held the sweatshirt up for them to see.

"You should bring it to Avalon," Mom said, misunderstanding my reason for coming in there. "As a memento to your past."

I didn't respond.

Instead, I looked to Mira.

"John Astor died on the Titanic," I said, and she nodded. "Our school was never called John Astor High."

"What's John Astor High?" Mom asked.

"What's the name of the street we live on?" I asked in

return, since for me, it had always been John Astor Road.

"The Great Ocean Road…" She sounded baffled, and she looked to Mira. "What's going on?"

Mira smirked and met my gaze.

Then we both looked at Mom, said, "time travel" in unison, and I walked back to my room to continue packing.

56

GEMMA

SATURDAY, JANUARY 1 (FIVE AND A HALF MONTHS LATER)

The day of my and Mira's eighteenth birthday was finally here. Well, the night, since we were born at 10:04 PM.

For our seventeenth birthday, we hadn't known for sure that we'd receive magic. I'd had faith, but that was all it had been—trusting my inner senses.

Now, as I stood with Mira, Ethan, William, Hypatia, and Darius in the desert outside the dragon kingdom, I had a similar feeling. Because at age eighteen, as long as they were in Ember, dragons shifted for the first time.

While Mira and I weren't full dragons, and we'd possibly never be able to shift, I held on to the hope that we'd be able to do this.

The ceremony wasn't as elaborate as the one where we'd received our magic at the cove. In fact, there wasn't a ceremony at all. We just had to stand there, wait for the time of our birth, and see what happened.

Ethan and I stood off to the side, gazing up at the full moon.

"Make a wish," he said softly.

I closed my eyes and did as he said, since wishes made on full moons always felt more powerful than wishes on stars.

Of course, I didn't tell him what I'd wished for, and he didn't ask. He didn't have to. Because right now, we both wanted the same thing.

Rebuilding the dragon kingdom had been going relatively smoothly so far. The fact that our people could control the elements had helped us get a framework in place way faster than it would have otherwise.

Since I was Ethan's twin flame, they respected me as their queen. But the feeling that I wasn't one of them never went away.

The feeling hit the hardest whenever Ethan and the others shifted and I couldn't.

"It's almost time," I said. "We should join the others."

"In a minute," he said. "First, a kiss for good luck."

Then his lips were on mine, and I savored this moment between us, like I did *every* moment between us.

"I love you," I said after pulling away.

"You know I love you," he said, and I smiled, since it was true. Deep down, I'd always known Ethan loved me, and I knew he always would.

Just as I'd always love him.

I glanced over at where Mira and William were standing across the way, staring at each other with as deep of a love as me and Ethan. William had succeeded in becoming Nephilim, and while he and Mira lived on Avalon, he'd come with her for the big night.

"Come on," I said to Ethan, reaching for his hand to lead him toward where Hypatia and Darius were standing. "It's time."

Mira and William joined us, and the six of us stood in a circle.

"One more minute," Hypatia said, as if Mira and I needed someone to inform us of the time. "We need to spread out to give the two of you space."

Ethan gave my hand one final squeeze for luck, then backed up with the others.

I glanced over at Mira—my twin looked positively magical with the crystals of her Crown glimmering in the moonlight.

"We've got this," she said, and I couldn't help but chuckle.

"You sure sound confident for someone who didn't even believe in magic a year ago," I said.

"That was then," she said. "This is now."

I nodded, understanding what she meant. The people we'd been a year ago felt nearly unrecognizable to who we were now. I felt as disconnected to the pre-magic version of myself as I did to the timelines I'd written over in my journeys to the past.

We stepped away from each other, creating ample room for what was hopefully coming next.

The seconds counted down in my head.

Five, four, three, two...

I was looking into my twin's eyes as magic roared inside me, throwing me into the air as my body exploded into its dragon form. And all at once, I felt complete.

Because I was a witch.

I was a dragon.

I was the Queen of Pentacles.

And now, finally, my magic was whole.

FROM THE AUTHOR

I hope you enjoyed the final book of the Dragon Twins series—which is also the final book in the Dark World: Four Queens (well, eight Queens) storyline.

This series has been such an adventure to write, especially when I mixed in time travel, which made me push myself harder than ever. I hope the *Back to the Future* fans out there caught my many references to the movies.

To chat with me and other readers about the book, go to www.facebook.com/groups/michellemadow and join my Facebook group now! I love hanging out with you all in there.

Also, make sure you never miss a new release by signing up to get emails and/or texts when my books come out!

Sign up for emails: michellemadow.com/subscribe

Sign up for texts: michellemadow.com/texts

If you enjoyed the *Dragon Twins* series, I'd love if you left a review on Amazon. The more positive reviews I have, the more encouraged I am to write my next book faster!

A review for the first book in the series, *The Dragon Twins,* is the most helpful. Go to mybook.to/dragontwins to leave your review now!

If you haven't read the other three series' in the Dark World universe, I recommend going back and reading them to get the full scope of the Four Queens story. Here are the links:

The Vampire Wish (Annika's story): mybook.to/vampirewish

The Angel Trials (Raven's story): mybook.to/angeltrials

The Faerie Games (Selena's story): mybook.to/faeriegames

If you enjoyed the Dark World series, then you'll love the Elementals series, which was my first series to hit it big! CLICK HERE or go to mybook.to/elementals1 to grab *Elementals* on Amazon, or turn the page to check out the cover and description.

ELEMENTALS: THE PROPHECY OF SHADOWS

MAGIC. ROMANCE. ADVENTURE.

Experience the *now completed* bestselling series that fans of *Harry Potter* and *Percy Jackson* are raving about.

"A must read!"
--USA Today

* A Top 100 Amazon Bestseller in the entire Kindle Store *

Nicole Cassidy is nervous about her first day at a new school. She's worried about her outfit. And her hair. She's imagined the teacher introducing her to the class, only to hear snickers around the room.

It turns out, things at her new school are going to be a lot harder than that. At Kinsley High, there's something new on the curriculum: magic.

It's not just the other students who have magic. So does Nicole.

She's a witch.

Not only is she a witch, she's descended from Greek gods.

It's almost too much for her to process. Luckily, one of her new classmates is more than happy to take her under his wing to teach her how to use her magic. His name is Blake, and he's sort of her type: mysterious, possibly trouble.

The connection between Nicole and Blake is instant. There's just one problem: Blake has a girlfriend, Danielle. Rumor has it she harbors a penchant for using dark magic. Especially on anyone who gets near Blake.

As Nicole tries to navigate her mysterious new school--and stay out of Danielle's crosshairs--a new threat emerges: the Olympian Comet. The comet hasn't been seen for thousands of years, and it's about to change everything.

With the Olympian Comet burning bright across the night sky, Nicole's sleepy town is turned upside down. Ancient monsters emerge, wreaking havoc on everyone and everything.

An ancient prophecy may hold the key to stopping the monsters and surviving the comet, but time is running out. As Nicole and her new classmates race to unravel the clues left by the prophecy, they soon learn that it's not just their town that's in danger. The Olympian Comet may be far more deadly than they ever imagined.

Start the adventure today and escape into this world of magic, romance, and mythology!

This five book series has been a perennial bestseller since its publication and has garnered over 2,000 reviews on Amazon, 10,000+ ratings on Goodreads, and millions of pages read in Kindle Unlimited.

Get it now at:
mybook.to/elementals1

Or turn the page to read the first four chapters!

ELEMENTALS

THE PROPHECY OF SHADOWS

1

The secretary fumbled through the stacks of papers on her desk, searching for my schedule. "Here it is." She pulled out a piece of paper and handed it to me. "I'm Mrs. Dopkin. Feel free to come to me if you have any questions."

"Thanks." I looked at the schedule, which had my name on the top, and listed my classes and their locations. "This can't be right." I held it closer, as if that would make it change. "It has me in all honors classes."

She frowned and clicked around her computer. "Your schedule is correct," she said. "Your homeroom teacher specifically requested that you be in the honors courses."

"But I wasn't in honors at my old school."

"It doesn't appear to be a mistake," she said. "And the

late bell's about to ring, so if you need a schedule adjustment, come back at the end of the day so we can discuss it. You're in Mr. Faulkner's homeroom, in the library. Turn right out of the office and walk down the hall. You'll see the library on the right. Go inside and head all the way to the back. Your homeroom is in the only door there. Be sure to hurry—you don't want to be late."

She returned to her computer, apparently done talking to me, so I thanked her for her help and left the office.

Kinsley High felt cold compared to my school in Georgia, and not just in the literal sense. Boxy tan lockers lined every wall, and the concrete floor was a strange mix of browns that reminded me of throw-up. The worst part was that there were no windows anywhere, and therefore a serious lack of sunlight.

I preferred the warm green carpets and open halls at my old school. Actually I preferred everything about my small Georgia town, especially the sprawling house and the peach tree farm I left behind. But I tried not to complain too much to my parents.

After all, I remembered the way my dad had bounced around the living room while telling us about his promotion to anchorman on the news station. It was his dream job, and he didn't mind that the only position available was in Massachusetts. My mom had jumped on board with the plan to move, confident that her paintings would sell better in a town closer to a major city. My younger sister Becca had liked the idea of starting fresh, along with how the shopping in Boston apparently exceeded anything in our town in Georgia.

There had to be something about the move for me to like. Unfortunately, I had yet to find it.

I didn't realize I'd arrived at the library until the double doors were in front of me. At least I'd found it without getting lost.

I walked inside the library, pleased to find it was nothing like the rest of the school. The golden carpet and wooden walls were warm and welcoming, and the upstairs even had windows. I yearned to run toward the sunlight, but the late bell had already rung, so I headed to the back of the library. Hopefully being new would give me a free pass on being late.

Just as the secretary had said, there was only one door. But with it's ancient peeling wood, it looked like it led to a storage room, not a classroom. And there was no glass panel, so I couldn't peek inside. I had to assume this was it.

I wrapped my fingers around the doorknob, my hand trembling. *It's your first day*, I reminded myself. *No one's going to blame you for being late on your first day.*

I opened the door, halfway expecting it to be a closet full of old books or brooms. But it wasn't a closet.

It was a classroom.

Everyone stared at me, and I looked to the front of the room, where a tall, lanky man in a tweed suit stood next to a blackboard covered with the morning announcements. His gray hair shined under the light, and his wrinkled skin and warm smile reminded me more of a grandfather than a teacher.

He cleared his throat and rolled a piece of chalk in his palm. "You must be Nicole Cassidy," he said.

"Yeah." I nodded and looked around at the other students. There were about thirty of them, and there seemed to be an invisible line going down the middle of the room, dividing them in half. The students near the door wore jeans and sweatshirts, but the ones closer to the wall looked like they were dressed for a fashion show instead of school.

"It's nice to meet you Nicole." The teacher sounded sincere, like he was meeting a new friend instead of a student. "Welcome to our homeroom. I'm Mr. Faulkner, but please call me Darius." He turned to the chalkboard, lifted his hand, and waved it from one side to the other. "You probably weren't expecting everything to look so normal, but we have to be careful. As I'm sure you know, we can't risk letting anyone else know what goes on in here."

Then the board shimmered—like sunlight glimmering off the ocean—and the morning announcements changed into different letters right in front of my eyes.

2

I BLINKED a few times to make sure I wasn't hallucinating. What I'd just seen couldn't have been real.

At least the board had stopped shimmering, although instead of the morning announcements, it was full of information about the meanings of different colors. I glanced at the other students, and while a few of them smiled, they were mostly unfazed. They just watched me, waiting for me to say something. Darius also stood calmly, waiting for my reaction.

"How did you do that?" I finally asked.

"It's easy," Darius said. "I used magic. Well, a task like that wouldn't have been easy for you, since you're only in your second year of studies, but given enough practice you'll get the hang of it." He motioned to a seat in the second row, next to a girl with chin-length mousy brown hair. "Please sit down, and we'll resume class."

I stared at him, not moving. "You used ... magic," I repeated, the word getting stuck in my throat. I looked around the room again, waiting for someone to laugh. This had to be a joke. After all, an owl hadn't dropped a letter down my fireplace to let me know I'd been accepted into a special school, and I certainly hadn't taken an enchanted train to get to Kinsley High. "Funny. Now tell me what you *really* did."

"You mean you don't know?" Darius's forehead crinkled.

"Is this a special studies homeroom?" I asked. "And I somehow got put into one about ... magic tricks?"

"It wasn't a trick," said an athletic boy in the center of the room. His sandy hair fell below his ears, and he leaned back in his seat, pushing his sleeves up to his elbows. "Why use tricks when we can do the real thing?"

I stared at him blankly and backed towards the door. He couldn't be serious. Because magic—*real* magic—didn't exist. They must be playing a joke on me. Make fun of the new kid who hadn't grown up in a town so close to Salem.

I wouldn't fall for it. So I might as well play along.

"If that was magic, then where are your wands?" I

held up a pretend wand, making a swooshing motion with my wrist.

Darius cleaned his glasses with the bottom of his sweater. "I'd assumed you'd already started your lessons at your previous school." He frowned and placed his glasses back on. "From your reaction, I'm guessing that's not the case. I apologize for startling you. Unfortunately, there's no easy way to say this now, so I might as well be out with it." He took a deep breath, and said, "We're witches. You are, too. And regarding your question, we don't use wands because real witches don't need them. That's an urban legend created by humans who felt safer believing that they couldn't be harmed if there was no wand in sight."

"You can't be serious." I laughed nervously and pulled at the sleeves of my sweater. "Even if witches did exist—which they don't—I'm definitely not one of them."

The only thing "magical" that had ever happened to me was how the ligament I tore in my knee while playing tennis last month had healed right after moving here. The doctor had said it was a medical miracle.

But that didn't make it *magic*.

"I am completely serious," Darius said. "We're all witches, as are you. And this *is* a special studies homeroom—it's for the witches in the school. Although of course the administration doesn't know that." He chuckled. "They just think it's for highly gifted students. Now, please take a seat in the chair next to Kate, and I'll explain more."

I looked around the room, waiting for someone to end this joke. But the brown-haired girl who I assumed was Kate tucked her hair behind her ears and studied her hands. The athletic boy next to her watched me expectantly, and smiled when he caught me looking at him. A girl behind him glanced through her notes, and several other students shuffled in their seats.

My sweater felt suddenly constricting, and I swallowed away the urge to bolt out of there. This was a mistake, and I had to fix it. Now.

"I'm going to go back to the office to make sure they gave me the right schedule," I said, pointing my thumb at the door. "They must have put me in the wrong homeroom. But have fun talking about…" I looked at the board again to remind myself what it said. "Energy colors and their meanings."

They were completely out of their minds.

I hurried out of the classroom, feeling like I could breathe again once I was in the library lobby. No one else was around, and I sat in a chair to collect my thoughts. I would go back to the front office in a minute. For now, I browsed through my cell phone, wanting to see something familiar to remind myself that I wasn't going crazy.

Looking through my friends' recent photos made me miss home even more. My eyes filled with tears at the thought of them living their lives without me. It hadn't been a week, and they'd already stopped texting me as often as usual. I was hundreds of miles away, and they were moving on, forgetting about me.

Not wanting anyone to see me crying, I wiped away the tears and switched my camera to front facing view to check my reflection. My eyes were slightly red, but not enough that anyone would notice. And my makeup was still intact.

I was about to put my phone away when I noticed something strange. The small scar above my left eyebrow—the one I'd gotten in fourth grade when I'd fallen on a playground—had disappeared. I brushed my index finger against the place where the indentation had been, expecting it to be a trick of the light. But the skin was soft and smooth.

As if the scar had never been there at all.

I dropped my hand down to my lap. Scars didn't disappear overnight, just like torn ligaments didn't repair themselves in days. And Darius had sounded so convinced that what he'd been saying was true. All of the students seemed to support what he was saying, too.

What if they actually believed what he was telling me? That magic *did* exist?

The thought was entertaining, but impossible. So I clicked out of the camera, put the phone back in my bag, and stood up. I had to get out of here. Maybe once I did, I would start thinking straight again.

"Nicole!" someone called from behind me. "Hold on a second."

I let out a long breath and turned around. The brown-haired girl Darius had called Kate was jogging in my direction. She was shorter than I'd originally thought, and the splattering of freckles across her nose made her look the same age as my younger sister Becca, who was in eighth grade. But that was where the similarities between Kate and Becca ended. Because Kate was relatively plain looking, except for her eyes, which were a unique shade of bright, forest green.

"I know that sounded crazy in there," she said once she reached me. She picked at the side of her thumbnail, and while I suspected she wanted me to tell her that it didn't sound crazy, I couldn't lie like that.

"Yeah. It did." I shifted my feet, gripping the strap of my bag. "I know this is Massachusetts and witches are a part of the history here, so if you all believe in that stuff, that's fine. But it's not really my sort of thing."

"Keep your voice down." She scanned the area, but

there was no one else in the library, so we were in the clear. "What Darius told you is real. How else would you explain what you saw in there, when he changed what was on the board?"

"A projector?" I shrugged. "Or maybe the board is a TV screen?"

"There's no projector." She held my gaze. "And the board isn't a television screen, even though that would be cool."

"Then I don't know." I glanced at the doors. "But magic wouldn't be on my list of explanations. No offense or anything."

"None taken," she said in complete seriousness. "But you were put in our homeroom for a reason. You're one of us. Think about it ... do strange things ever happen to you or people around you? Things that have no logical explanation?"

I opened my mouth, ready to say no, but closed it. After all, two miraculous healings in a few days definitely counted as strange, although I wouldn't go so far as to call it *magic*.

But wasn't that the definition of a miracle—something that happened without any logical explanation, caused by something bigger than us? Something *magical*?

"It has." Kate smiled, bouncing on her toes. "Hasn't it?"

"I don't know." I shrugged, not wanting to tell her the specifics. It sounded crazy enough in my head—how would it sound when spoken out loud? "But I guess I'll go back with you for now. Only because the secretary said she won't adjust my schedule until the end of the day, anyway."

She smiled and led the way back to the classroom. Everyone stared at me again when we entered, and I didn't meet anyone's eyes as I took the empty chair next to her.

Darius nodded at us and waited for everyone to settle down. Once situated, I finally glanced around at the other students. The boy Darius had called Chris smiled at me, a girl with platinum hair filed her nails under the table, and the girl next to her looked like she was about to fall asleep. They were all typical high school students waiting for class to end.

But my eyes stopped at the end of the row on a guy with dark shaggy hair. His designer jeans and black leather jacket made him look like he'd come straight from a modeling shoot, and the casual way he leaned back in his chair exuded confidence and a carefree attitude. Then his gaze met mine, and goosebumps rose over my skin. His eyes were a startling shade of burnt brown, and they were soft, but calculating. Like he was trying to figure me out.

Kate rested an elbow on the table and leaned closer to me. "Don't even think about it," she whispered, and I yanked my gaze away from his, my cheeks flushing at the realization that I'd been caught staring at him. "That's Blake Carter. He's been dating Danielle Emerson since last year. She's the one to his left."

Not wanting to stare again, I glanced at Danielle from the corner of my eye. Her chestnut hair was supermodel thick, her ocean blue eyes were so bright that I wondered if they were colored contacts, and her black v-neck shirt dropped as low as possible without being overly inappropriate for school.

Of course Blake had a girlfriend, and she was beautiful. I never stood a chance.

"As I said earlier, we're going to review the energy colors and what they mean," Darius said, interrupting my thoughts. "But before we begin, who can explain to Nicole how we use energy?"

I sunk down in my seat, hating that the attention had been brought back to me. Luckily, the athletic boy next to Kate who'd said the thing earlier about magic not being a trick raised his hand.

"Chris," Darius called on him. "Go ahead."

Chris pushed his hair off his forehead and faced me.

His t-shirt featured an angry storm cloud holding a lighting bolt like a baseball bat, with "Trenton Thunder" written below it. It was goofy, and not a sports team that I'd ever heard of. But his boyish grin and rounded cheeks made him attractive in a cute way. Not in the same "stop what you're doing because I'm walking in your direction" way as Blake, but he definitely would have gotten attention from the girls at my old school.

"There's energy everywhere." Chris moved his hands in a giant arc above his head to demonstrate. "Humans know that energy exists—they've harnessed it for electronics. The difference between us and humans is that we have the power to tap into energy and use it ourselves, and humans don't." He smiled at me, as if I was supposed to understand what he meant. "Make sense?"

"Not really," I said. "Sorry."

"It's easier if you relate it to something familiar," he said, speaking faster. "What happens to the handle of a metal spoon when you leave it in boiling water?"

"It gets hot?" I said it as a question. This was stuff people learned in fifth grade science—not high school homeroom.

"And what happens when it's plastic?"

"It doesn't get hot," I said slowly. "It stays room temperature."

"Exactly." He grinned at me like I'd just solved an astrophysics mathematical equation. "Humans are like plastic. Even if they're immersed in energy, they can't conduct it. Witches are like metal. We have the ability to absorb energy and control it as we want."

"So, how do we take in this energy?" I asked, since I might as well humor him.

"Through our hands." Chris turned his palms up, closed his eyes, and took a deep breath. He looked like a meditating Buddha. Students snickered, and Chris re-opened his eyes, pushed his sleeves up, and sat back in his chair.

"O-o-kay." I elongated the word, smiling and laughing along with everyone else.

Darius cleared his throat, and everyone calmed down. "We can conduct energy from the Universe into our bodies," he said, his voice full of authority. Chills passed through me, and even though I still didn't believe any of this, I sat back to listen. "Once we've harnessed it, we can use it as we like. Think of energy like light. It contains different colors, each relating to an aspect of life. I've written them on the board. The most basic exercise we learn in this class is to sense this energy and absorb it. Just open your mind, envision the color you're focusing on, and picture it entering your body through your palms."

I rotated my hand to look at my palm. It looked normal—not like it was about to open up and absorb energy from the Universe.

"We're going to do a meditation session," Darius continued. "Everyone should pick a color from the board and picture it as energy entering your palms. Keep it simple and absorb the energy—don't push it back out into the Universe. This exercise is for practice and self-improvement." He looked at me, a hint of challenge in his eyes. "Now, please pick a color and begin."

I looked around the room to see what others were doing. Most people already had their eyes closed, the muscles in their faces calm and relaxed. They were really getting into this. As if they truly believed it.

If I didn't at least *look* like I was trying, I would stand out—again. So I might as well go along with it and pretend.

I re-examined the board and skimmed through the "meanings" of the colors. Red caught my attention first. It apparently increased confidence, courage, and love, along with attraction and desire. The prospect made me glance at Blake, who sat still with his eyes closed, his lips set in a line of concentration.

But he was out of my league *and* he had a girlfriend. I shouldn't waste my time hoping for anything to happen between us.

Instead, I read through the other colors and settled on green. It supposedly brought growth, success, and luck, along with helping a person open their mind, become more aware of options, and choose a good path. Those were all things I needed right now.

I opened my palms towards the ceiling and closed my eyes. Once comfortable, I steadied my breathing and tried clearing my mind.

Then there was the question of how to "channel" a color. Picturing it seemed like a good start, so I imagined myself pulling green out of the air, the color glowing with life. A soft hum filled my ears as it expanded and pushed against me, like waves crashing over my skin. The palms of my hands tingled, and the energy flowed through my body, joining with my blood as it pumped through my veins. It streamed up my arms, moved down to my stomach, and poured down to my toes. Green glowed behind my eyelids, and I kept gathering it and gathering it until it grew so much that it had nowhere else to go.

Then it pushed its way out of my palms with such force that it must have lit up the entire room.

3

The bell rang, and my eyes snapped open, the classroom coming into focus. I looked around, taking in the scuffed tiled floor, the chalkboard covered with writing, the white plaster walls, and the lack of windows. Everything looked normal. Unchanged. There was no proof that anything I'd just felt had been more than a figment of my imagination.

But that energy flowing through my body had been so *real*. I tightened my hands into fists and opened them back up, but only a soft tingle remained. Then it disappeared completely.

Kate stood up, dropped her backpack on her chair, and studied me. "I'm guessing from the look on your face that it worked," she said.

"I don't know." I shrugged and picked up my bag.

"I'm not sure what was supposed to happen." I met her eyes and managed a small smile, since it wasn't exactly a lie.

But the energy I'd felt around me was unlike anything I'd ever experienced. Which meant my imagination was running out of control. Because there was no proof that I'd done anything. What I'd "experienced" had existed only in my head. Right?

Kate glanced at her watch. "What class do you have first?"

I pulled out my schedule. "Honors Biology." I scrunched my nose at the prospect. "They put me in all honors classes, and I have no idea why. I was in regular classes at my old school."

"I've got Honors Bio, too," she said. "Come on. I'll explain the whole honors thing on the way there."

I followed Kate down the hallway, although I kept bumping into people, since my mind was spinning after what had happened in homeroom. I'd felt something during that meditation session. Maybe it was the energy that Darius was talking about. And if this energy stuff *was* the reason behind the miraculous recovery of my torn tendon and the healed scar ...

I pushed the thought away. There had to be another explanation. One that made *sense*.

Kate edged closer to the wall to give me space to

walk next to her. "So, about the honors classes," she said, lowering her voice. "You saw what was written on the board. Each color has a different meaning. Once we learn how to harness energy properly, we can use the different colors to help us ... do things."

"What kind of things?" I asked.

"Let's take yellow—my personal favorite—as an example," she said. "Yellow increases focus and helps us remember information. If you channel yellow energy before studying for a test, it won't take as long to review everything, and you'll remember more. It'll make your memory almost photographic. Pretty cool, right?"

"It does sound useful," I agreed. "Although I'm still not buying all this colors and energy stuff."

"Give it time." Kate smiled, as if she knew something I didn't, and stopped in front of a classroom door. "We're here. Want to sit with me?" She led the way to a table in the front, and I followed, even though front and center wasn't my thing. "I'll help you with the basics after school," she offered. "You got the hang of channeling energy pretty quickly, so it shouldn't be hard. Sometimes it takes the freshmen months to gather enough energy to feel anything significant. It was obvious from where I was sitting that you did it on your first try. That was pretty impressive."

"I'm not sure I actually did anything, but sure, I'll

study with you after school," I said. Even though this energy stuff sounded crazy, it was nice of Kate to reach out. I didn't want to miss the chance to make my first friend here. "I could definitely use help getting caught up with my classes."

"Great." Kate beamed. "I'm sure you'll pick it up quickly."

More students piled in, a few of them people I recognized from homeroom. Then, just as I'd started to think it was stupid to hope he would also be in this class, Blake strolled inside, with Danielle trailing close behind.

His eyes met mine, and my breath caught, taken aback by how he'd noticed me again. But he couldn't be interested in me like *that*. It was probably just because I was new. And because, as embarrassing as it was to admit, he'd caught me staring at him. So I opened my textbook to the chapter that Kate already had open, focusing on a section on dominant and recessive genes as if it were the most fascinating thing I'd ever read in my life.

"I told you in homeroom that he's taken, remember?" Kate whispered once Blake and Danielle were far enough away.

My cheeks heated. "Was it that obvious?"

"That you were checking him out?" Kate asked, and I

nodded, despite how humiliating it was that she'd noticed. "Yeah."

"I'm not doing it on purpose," I said. "I know that he has a girlfriend. I would never try anything, I promise. But … have you seen him? It was hard not to at least *look*."

"I know you're not doing it on purpose," she said. "He's one of the hottest guys in the school—I get that. But Danielle doesn't take it too kindly when girls flirt with Blake. Or check out Blake. Or even look like they're *interested* in Blake. It's in your best interest to keep your distance from both of them. Trust me."

I was about to ask why, but before I could, the bell rang and class began.

4

The other sophomores from homeroom were in most of my classes, and Kate sat with me in one, including lunch. I was so behind in the honors courses that I seriously needed whatever Kate said she would teach me after school to help.

"What class do you have next?" Kate asked as we packed our bags after advanced Spanish.

I pulled my schedule out of my pocket. "Ceramics." I groaned. I wasn't awful at art, but I would have preferred a music elective, since music was always my favorite class. "What about you?"

"Theatre," she answered, tucking her hair behind her ears. "I want to be in the school play this spring, but I always get nervous on stage. Hopefully the class will help."

"You'll get in," I said. "Besides, can't you use that witchy energy stuff to convince the teacher to give you the part you want? Or mess up other people during their auditions so they don't get the leads?"

Her eyes darted around the hall, and she leaned in closer, lowering her voice. "We don't use our powers to take advantage of others," she said. "I'll fill you in on everything later. Okay?"

I nodded and followed her through the art wing, resisting the urge to ask her more right now. Instead, I looked around. Student paintings decorated the walls, and what sounded like a flute solo came from a room close by. Kate stopped in front of the double doors that led to the theatre. "This is me," she said. "The ceramics room is upstairs—you shouldn't miss it."

We split ways, and like Kate had told me, the ceramics room was easy to find. Kilns lined the side wall, pottery wheels were on the other end, bricks of clay were stacked in shelves in the back, and the huge windows were a welcome change from the stuffy classrooms I'd been in so far.

I looked around to see if anyone seemed receptive to having the new girl join them, and my eyes stopped when they reached Blake's. He sat at the table furthest away, leaning back in his seat with his legs outstretched. The chairs next to him were empty. He nodded at me, as if acknowledging me as a member of a special club, and I noticed that no one else from homeroom was in this class. Could he be inviting me to sit with him?

Since everyone from homeroom seemed to stick together, I took that as a yes and walked toward Blake's table, my pulse quickening with every step. I remembered what Kate had told me earlier about Danielle—how she was crazy possessive over Blake—but Danielle wasn't here. And Blake was the only person who wanted me to join him. Refusing would be rude.

He moved his legs to give me room, and I settled in the seat next to him. His deep, liquid eyes had various shades of reddish brown running through them, and he was watching me as if he was waiting for me to say something. I swallowed, not sure how to start, and settled on the obvious.

"Hi." My heart pounded so hard I feared he could hear it. "You're in my homeroom, right?"

"Yep," he said smoothly. "We also have biology, history, and Spanish together." He counted off each on his fingers. "And given that you're in Darius's homeroom, it's safe to say that you have Greek mythology with me next period as well. I'm Blake."

"Nicole," I introduced myself, even though Darius had already done so in front of the class this morning. "I heard that all of the sophomores in our homeroom have to take Greek mythology. Luckily I read *The Odyssey* in English last year, so I shouldn't be totally lost."

"There's a reason we're required to take Greek mythology." He scooted closer to me, as if about to tell me a secret, and I leaned forward in anticipation. "Did you know that we—meaning everyone in our homeroom—are descended from the Greek gods?"

I arched an eyebrow. "Like Zeus and all of them living in a castle on the clouds?" I asked.

"Exactly." He smirked. "Except that they're referred to as the Olympians, and they call their 'castle in the clouds' Mount Olympus."

"So you're saying that we're *gods*?"

"We're not gods." He smiled and shook his head. "But we have 'diluted god blood' in us. It's what gives us our powers."

"Right." I wasn't sure how else to respond, and I looked down at the table. Was he playing a joke on me? Trying to see how gullible the new kid could be?

"What's wrong?" He watched me so intensely—so seriously—that I knew he was truly concerned.

"The truth?" I asked, and he nodded, his gaze locked on mine. So I took a deep breath, and said, "Everything from our homeroom sounds crazy to me. But you're all so serious about it that I'm starting to think you actually believe it."

"It's a lot to take in at once," he said.

"That's the understatement of the day." I flaked a piece of dried clay off the table with my thumbnail. "But Kate offered to teach me some stuff after school, and she's been really nice by taking me around all day, so I told her I would listen to her."

"Kate's a rule follower," Blake said, crossing his arms. "She's only going to tell you about a fraction of the stuff we can do. But stay in homeroom with us, and maybe my friends and I will show you how to have *real* fun with our abilities."

The teacher walked inside before I could respond, and the chattering in the room quieted. As much as I wanted to ask Blake what he meant, I couldn't right now. We weren't supposed to talk about our abilities when humans could hear.

Then I realized: I'd thought of other people as "humans," like I wasn't one of them anymore.

The scary thing was—I might be starting to believe it.

Keep reading Elementals!

Get it now at:

mybook.to/elementals1

ABOUT THE AUTHOR

Michelle Madow is a USA Today bestselling author of fast-paced, young adult fantasy novels full of magic, adventure, romance, and twists you'll never see coming. She's sold over two million books worldwide and has been translated into multiple languages.

Michelle grew up in Maryland, and now lives in Florida. She wrote her first book in her junior year of college and hasn't stopped writing since! She also loves traveling, and has been to all seven continents. Someday, she hopes to travel the world for a year on a cruise ship.

Never miss a new release by signing up to get emails or texts when Michelle's books come out:

Sign up for emails: michellemadow.com/subscribe
Sign up for texts: michellemadow.com/texts

Connect with Michelle:

Facebook Group: facebook.com/groups/michellemadow
Instagram: @michellemadow
Email: michelle@madow.com
Website: www.michellemadow.com

THE DRAGON QUEEN

Published by Dreamscape Publishing

Copyright © 2021 Michelle Madow

ASIN: B092MXCNR2
ISBN: 9798471684874

This book is a work of fiction. Though some actual towns, cities, and locations may be mentioned, they are used in a fictitious manner and the events and occurrences were invented in the mind and imagination of the author. Any similarities of characters or names used within to any person past, present, or future is coincidental.

All rights reserved. No part of this book may be used or reproduced in any manner whatsoever without written permission from the author. Brief quotations may be embodied in critical articles or reviews.

❦ Created with Vellum

Printed in Great Britain
by Amazon